AGNES SAM was born in 1942, the great-granddaughter of indentured labourers from India who were shipped to South Africa in the nineteenth century. She was brought up in Port Elizabeth, and had a Catholic education. She attended university at Roma, Lesotho and Zimbabwe and taught science in Zambia. In 1973 she was exiled from South Africa and came to England, where she studied English Literature at the University of York. She revisited South Africa twenty years later, in 1993, to attend South Africa's first conference on democracy and academic freedom, held at Fort Hare University. A number of her stories have been published in periodicals and anthologies, and she has had two plays broadcast on BBC Radio 4. She now lives in York.

Jesus is Indian and Other Short Stories is her first published volume.

AGNES SAM

JESUS IS INDIAN

and Other Stories

Heinemann

Heinemann Educational Publishers
A Division of Heinemann Publishers (Oxford) Ltd
Halley Court, Jordan Hill, Oxford OX2 8EJ

Heinemann: A Division of Reed Publishing (USA) Inc.
361 Hanover Street, Portsmouth, NH 03801–3912, USA

Heinemann Educational Books (Nigeria) Ltd
PMB 5205, Ibadan
Heinemann Educational Boleswa
PO box 10103, Village Post Office, Gaborone, Botswana

FLORENCE   PRAGUE   PARIS   MADRID
ATHENS   MELBOURNE   JOHANNESBURG
AUCKLAND   SINGAPORE   TOKYO
CHICAGO   SAO PAULO

Series Editor: Adewale Maja-Pearce

British Library Cataloguing in Publication Data
A catalogue record for this book is available from the British Library.

Cover design by Touchpaper
Cover illustration by Amanda Ward
Author photographed by Jason Chinnian

ISBN 0435 909215

Phototypeset by CentraCet Limited, Cambridge
Printed and bound in Great Britain
by Cox and Wyman Ltd, Reading, Berkshire

94 95 96   12 11 10 9 8 7 6 5 4 3 2 1

Hama
Uncle Benny Auntie Violet
Auntie Millie

Grateful acknowledgment is made to the following for
permission to reprint copyright material:
Dangaroo Press, Denmark for *Poppy*, first published in *Kunapipi*, vol. VI,
No. 1, 1984, and for *The Seed*, first published in *Kunapipi*, Vol. VII,
No. 1, 1985.
Konigshausen und Neuman, Würzburg, West Germany for *The Dove*, first
published in *The Story Must Be Told*, edited by Peter O. Stummer, 1986.
Sheba Feminist Publishers, London for *The Seed*, published in *Charting the
Journey* edited by Shabnam Grewal, Jackie Kay, Liliane Landor, Gail
Lewis and Pratibha Parma, 1988.
Oxford University Press for the extract from 'God's Grandeur' by Gerard
Manley Hopkins.

Grateful acknowledgment is made to Hugh Tinker whose *A
New System of Slavery* documents the facts handed down
through oral history.

Contents

Introduction

It was not until after my grandfather's death in South Africa, while we were sorting through his papers, that we made a discovery suggesting the truth of stories we had been told: my great-grandfather was shanghaied as a child from India to South Africa in the nineteenth century.

The discovery brought with it the immediate realisation that the history of Indians in South Africa was suppressed. For, as a schoolgirl in Port Elizabeth, I was taught a history beginning with a Portuguese sailor in the fifteenth century roughing the seas in search of a spice route to India. Bartholomeu Dias, Vasco da Gama, the Van der Stels, the Dutch settlers with Jan van Riebeeck, the 5,000 British settlers in 1820, even details about a tiny group of 150 French Huguenots fleeing religious persecution in France, all figured in this history. But how and why the largest group of Indians outside the subcontinent came to be in South Africa was never accounted for.

The papers we found document my great-grandfather's arrival in Durban on the *Lord George Bentinck II* on 24 December 1860. They record his release from indentureship in 1913. The release document gives his age as sixty-two. This means that he was nine years old when he arrived in Durban in 1860. Bearing in mind that his exact age on arrival, even on release, may be inaccurate, what is indisputable is that he remained in indenture from 1860 until 1913 – that is for fifty-three years. My great-grandfather is registered 'son of Veerasamy'. We found no records suggesting that his father accompanied him.

Since that discovery I have identified the *Lord George Bentinck II* as the first ship to carry indentured labourers from India to South Africa in the nineteenth century. And I now know indenture ended in 1911, two years before my great-grandfather was released.

My fascination with this discovery springs from the irony of being well versed in South African history, while my own was kept from me; and now I am in exile, the records I wish eagerly to examine are inaccessible.

It seemed reasonable to question this omission; to wonder if the presence of Indians on African soil was simply too insignificant for inclusion in South Africa's history; to query its irrelevance in a country where cheap labour is the foundation of the economy; and to pursue the significance of the Indian presence in South Africa, and its exclusion from the history books.

It occurred to me that within South Africa, without access to documents such as I discovered, similar questions might never be asked about African, Chinese, Coloured, and Malay history. Because it is essential for all South Africans, if we are to recuperate from the disease which apartheid spread amongst us, to appreciate that our history was not one of conquest, I searched for some answers regarding the Indians, always aware I might unearth details best left forgotten. It is my hope that others will take up the wider implications in relation to the other racial groups excluded from South African history.

And then, hitch-hiking through Central Africa, still intrigued by my discovery, I visited the Zimbabwe Ruins prior to Ian Smith's Unilateral Declaration of Independence. There I looked up in amazement at towering dry-stone walls and towers – and listened in disbelief to Rhodesians attributing the building of this place to Arabs, to Greeks, to the Portuguese, to anyone but the ancestors of the African people who lived there. This attitude reinforced my fears that our history was not merely unwritten, it was distorted where evidence – such as this impressive place of stones – could not be removed. (Artefacts from the Zimbabwe Ruins holding the secret about the people, were removed by the explorers who first discovered this place for Europe.)

Having only the year 1860 to go on, I looked for a recent international event that could have a bearing on labour, and unearthed the abolition of slavery in 1833. There was a connection.

The Dutch in the Cape had established their lifestyle on slavery, importing African slaves from Madagascar and Mozambique, and Malay slaves from Dutch colonies in the East Indies. By the time of the abolition in 1833, Cape Colony, by then a British possession, had 40,000 slaves.

The trade in slaves became illegal as early as 1807, but people were retained as slaves beyond 1833. The distinction between the two abolitions – the abolition of the slave trade, and the abolition of slavery – is essential to any later study of labour in South Africa. It establishes that although forbidden to sell slaves (the trade continued illegally), the condition of slavery continued for at least a further twenty-six years. It is the condition of slavery which research will show has been perpetuated into modern times under various names, because the demand for cheap labour did not abate once the trade and ownership of slaves was prohibited. In Cape Colony, the British selected a date in 1834 for the freeing of slaves. The date coincided with the Afrikaners' decision to trek from the Cape. In a document signed by Piet Retief, the Afrikaners listed the reasons for their decision to move away from British rule, of which one was the loss incurred as a result of the emancipation of slaves.

The Afrikaners trekked into Natal, attracting the interest of the British, who quickly extended their control to embrace the region, thus forcing the Afrikaners to trek further away.

Those who settled in Natal found the conditions ideal for growing sugar cane and again expected cheap labour for the sugar cane plantations. The Zulus, however, traditionally living and farming in Natal, refused to co-operate with the colonisers, hoping that failure of the sugar cane economy would lead the colonisers to leave. Their refusal forced the Natal government to approach India, which was still part of the British Empire. Gandhi was yet to be born.

For plantation owners prohibited from owning slaves, the solution became indenture: Indians would not come out to South Africa as slaves, but as indentured labourers. In colonial times an indenture was an 'official requisition for stores or goods from abroad'. It was also 'a document binding a person to a master' (OED). The indentured labourer was therefore the equivalent of inanimate goods requisitioned by a colonial person through the Colonial Office, and was also in bondage to a master until the period of indenture was over. Whether such goods would be entitled to human rights from a people who had recently believed in slave property is a matter for conjecture.

But nineteenth century Indians proved reluctant to leave India. Unlike their European contemporaries, Indians had no need to search for silks, spices, or sea routes to anywhere. Until the nineteenth century Indians never left India to work abroad in significant numbers, possibly because crossing the ocean was considered taboo by Hindus. Furthermore, no assurance was given that conditions under indenture would be any better than those for slaves. (A large proportion of the slaves in Mauritius were Indian.) It is hard to imagine illiterate Indian peasants arriving on the scene and being treated differently from slaves by the very plantation owners who were disgruntled at losing their slave property. In actual fact, following reports of ill-treatment in *The Times*, an official had later to be designated 'Protector of Immigrants' (Ordinance No. 13 of 1872).

Given the reluctance of Indians to leave India, men were employed to recruit labourers. These men, called kangani, received a commission for each labourer they recruited. Between the abolition of slavery and the abolition of indenture, close to two million Indians left India.

Each kangani travelled to the villages, made extravagant promises to the peasants about work and pay, and escorted them to the ports. Along the way the kangani provided food, clothing, and shelter. On arrival at the port recruits were placed in depots which proved to be the breeding ground for cholera and dysentery. Here many peasant labourers contracted and died of these diseases, or died on the voyage to South Africa. Those recruits who wished to opt out were expected to pay for the provisions they had received. Having no money, they were indebted to the kangani, and forced to proceed to Natal.

The majority, dreaming of returning to India as wealthy men, went without their families. They were Hindu and Muslim Hindi speakers, coming from Bengal, Bihar, Madhya Pradesh and Orissa. About five per cent were Christian. My great-grandfather's documents carry a Christian first name. Since he was a child, and alone, and there was a very strong missionary presence in Natal, it is difficult to know whether his conversion occurred in Natal or in India.

Women were more fearful of leaving India, perhaps because their situation would be vulnerable should they be widowed. Although the number of women who went was initially small, the proportion grew until it was actually stipulated that twenty-five women had to be recruited for every one hundred men. This condition, certainly to forestall problems of sexuality for the male labourers, offered scope for unscrupulous practices, such as abductions (see the *London Standard*, 5 April 1871). Women also fell easy prey to the kanganis if they were escaping a domestic or legal situation, or even if they were simply looking for work. Those who were tricked into going to a depot could only be released by a male relative. To protect themselves from sexual harassment at the depots, women entered into forms of liaisons with men, even before they set sail for South Africa.

In this climate of Indians unwilling to leave India, and of kanganis paid on a commission basis, my great-grandfather might have been kidnapped.

An expert I consulted could not verify the use of children as indentured labourers. And yet, the regulations governing the payment of indentured labourers provided a clue: there was a proviso that 'females and children under ten years of age' were to be paid half the adult male ration.

Parallels with slavery are obvious, except that in the case of indenture, a colonial government, in this instance the British Indian Government, and not a private trader, was exporting the labourers.

The aspect of slavery relevant to the suspected kidnapping of my great-grandfather follows from the fact that slavery, instead of ending abruptly with its abolition, was phased out. The abolition dictated that from the age of six years children of slaves had to work for seven years, while their owner could retain their wages. They were freed only after the seven year period (Cape of Good Hope Ordinance No. 1 of 1835). It became clear that the abolitionists, though opposing slavery, were not against child labour. Indentured children would have raised no protest in South Africa or from the international community. Recent news about child labour in India lends credence to the nineteenth-century reports.

When considering reasons for the suppression of Indian peasant history, one has to ask if a difference in the situation of

Indians in South Africa today, compared with their situation in the nineteenth-century, might have made it politic to erase the earlier history. Who would benefit from this suppression? The Indians themselves, or the political system of apartheid?

Nineteenth-century South Africa was composed of four distinct republics – Cape Colony, Natal, Transvaal Republic (South African Republic) and Orange River Sovereignty – each with its own governing body. Although destined for Natal, indentured Indians were subject to restricted immigration into each of the republics from the outset. They required permission to cross from one republic into another; they could be arrested for vagrancy if found outside the master's plantation; they were refused the right of settlement in Orange River Sovereignty and could only travel into the region if in transit. By 1897 an Act of Parliament made it essential for them to carry passes (Act 28 of 1897). All laws passed after 1860 – for example the Vagrancy Laws, the Pass Laws, and the Poll Tax – were designed to control the movement and to restrict the number of Indians in South Africa.

Until recently, a South African Indian could not spend more than twenty-four hours in the Orange Free State. In addition, the birth of a child to two Indian South Africans outside South Africa could not be registered with the Registry of Births: in effect the child could not be given South African nationality.

Twentieth-century South Africa is composed of four provinces and numerous Bantustans. The movement of Africans in and out of the Bantustans is severely restricted. Is it possible that some of the laws enacted in the nineteenth century to control Indians evolved to the present restrictions on the movement and rights of Africans?

We know that in the mines today African men are not allowed to have their families live with them; women working in service have to sleep on the premises whilst their families live in the townships. Referring back to the post-slavery period, the only group from outside Europe to enter South Africa (the Chinese entered later), were the Indians. Because indentured Indians were expected to return to India, their dependants were refused permission to join them in South Africa. Indentureship may be seen as the the first form of migrant labour in South Africa.

Initially for three years, the term of indenture was extended to five years, at the end of which time Indians were released and free to take up any other form of employment or return to India. If they renewed their contracts of indenture until they had served ten years, Indians could receive free passage to India or be given Crown land to the value of the passage home. (Some families in Natal still retain the original parchment deeds to the land they were given.)

To the consternation of the planters, however, most Indians did not renew their contracts, and once ex-indentured they stayed on in Natal. As a result they did not qualify for free passage to India. To make matters worse, those who did return to India complained to the Indian government of their treatment in Natal. Since only 6,000 Indian labourers had been introduced into Natal between 1860 and 1865, and indentured immigration ceased between 1865 and 1870, the planters once more had a labour problem.

Still keen to have Indians remain in indentureship for as long as possible, the settlers then demanded that labourers should not be allowed to settle in South Africa. To ensure both that indentured Indians continually renewed their contract of indentureship, and that they remained permanent foreigners in South Africa, the legal system was manipulated to maintain the servitude of indentured Indians. It became a condition that Indians would only be allowed to remain as free people in South Africa if they owned land. Some of the republics then enacted laws for the purpose of preventing Indians from purchasing land. At the end of a term of indentureship, Indians now had the option of returning to India only if they paid the return passage, failing which they were forced to sign on for a further period of indentureship.

The wages of indentured Indians, however, were not paid with any regularity. The money due was often held back for two months or for indefinite periods. As a rule it was forfeited for illness or absenteeism, and was withheld if work stopped for any reason. Few indentured Indians could therefore either purchase land or pay their passage to India.

In this situation of poverty, and in their fear of crossing the ocean, lie the reasons why the majority of Indians stayed on in South Africa, and not, as is so confidently proposed, in conditions in India. The disproportionately high number of suicides amongst the Indian labourers is an indication of their misery. And the fifty-three years my great-grandfather remained indentured, almost certainly unaware of the abolition, is evidence of their plight.

Prior to the end of indentureship in 1911, South Africa experienced the Anglo-Boer War, concentration camps, Gandhi's protest movement, the formation of the Indian National Congress, publication of the *Indian Opinion*, and the unification of the four republics into a Union of South Africa.

With the formation of the Union of South Africa, the laws and franchises peculiar to each of the four republics, instead of being repealed, remained in operation. Indians who had not moved out of Natal before the Union were restricted to living there. Despite the discovery of gold in the Transvaal and diamonds in the Cape, the continued restriction on the movement of Indians in and out of the four provinces meant that the booms had no effect on the prospects, or the standard of living, of the poorest group in South Africa at the time – the indentured Indians in Natal.

Not content with restricting their movement and taxing them, the government and the European establishment made several abortive attempts to remove Indians from South Africa once indentureship ended. Between 1914 and 1919 there were moves to repatriate them to India; in 1927 there were plans for assisted emigration from South Africa; in 1930 there were plans to resettle Indian South Africans in another part of the British Empire: British North Borneo, British Guiana, and British New Guinea were offered as settlement areas.

These moves are reminiscent of the settlement of freed slaves in Liberia, while repatriation with assisted passage is still suggested for Asians and Caribbeans in the United Kingdom today.

The right of settlement and the right to purchase land, both denied to Indians in the nineteenth century, are part of the intricacies of the Bantustan policy now in operation in South Africa. Except for a period in the nineteenth century when Africans could own land, the right to purchase land has always been denied to South Africa's African people. The significance of the right to purchase land and its implication with regard to the denial of civil rights for African people, is an area that should be researched, perhaps with reference to British and European history.

Indentured labour replaced slavery. Migrant labour replaced indentured labour. The Bantustans will replace migrant labour. The difference between these four forms of labour may have been only in the letter of the law. The labourers – slaves, indentured labourers, migrant workers and people in the Bantustans – shared the status of foreigners in South Africa. When after a period of years, the labourer had the right of settlement, laws were enacted to maintain the status of foreigner. Even when the labourer was *not* a foreigner, a law was created to *make* the labourer a 'foreigner': the Bantustan scheme is a shrewd manoeuvre to continue the practice of slave/indentured/ migrant labour, only this time using nationals and not foreigners. By depriving nationals of citizenship, they become 'foreigners' in the country of their birth. Whether its covert purpose is to concentrate African people in a confined area for purposes of control, or to phase out migrant labour now that most of Africa is independent, the Bantustans function as if black South Africans are migrant labourers in South Africa.

Throughout history, neighbouring countries have encroached upon each other's territories, but South Africa, by creating Bantustans, erodes itself, in a self-mutilating way.

Indians may have been excluded from South Africa's history because of the temporary status intended for them. They may even have considered themselves temporarily resident in South Africa – but their perception of their status is irrelevant to their exclusion from South African history.

Colin Bundy in *The Rise and Fall of the South African Peasantry* devotes two paragraphs to Indian peasants. Such marginal-isation can be rationalised. But it becomes a matter for concern where the marginalised group becomes an easily identifiable scapegoat, as Indians have become in South Africa. Placed as they are as a buffer between whites and Africans, they have been removed by the Group Areas Board to live in Indian areas sited between white suburbs and African townships, so that any violence erupting out of an African area will be dissipated amongst the Indians, thus safeguarding the whites.

Anti-Indian feeling in Natal dominated the early period of

Nationalist government. Attacks on Indians were feared to have
been encouraged by white racists in Natal, even by the police.

Today it is not unusual for Indians to request reclassification
as 'Coloured'.

Illiterate Indian peasants were introduced into a political
situation of which they were wholly ignorant. Transporting
people from India to work on the plantations effectively
frustrated the Zulus' attempt to bring about the failure of the
sugar cane economy. Yet, from another perspective, the intro-
duction of indentured labourers from India is testament to the
victory of Africans who refused to labour for the plantation
owners in Natal.

Both Africans and Indians, by speaking English, wearing
western clothes, even accepting conversion to Christianity,
adapted to the language, religion and customs of the colonisers.
Yet only these two groups were restricted from participating in
the booms which followed both the gold and diamond rushes in
South Africa.

Indian women were essential to the process of adaptation.
They confronted new school systems for their children; struggled
to maintain the old religion in a new country; faced prohibitions
about marriage that further restricted the limited number of
suitors from the same religious background, language group or
caste. They experienced indentured labour; discriminatory
laws; a poll tax and imprisonment when they could not pay;
isolation from their families in India; and even the unwanted
attentions of European men:

> . . . the women, with their flashing eyes, with their half-
> covered, well-formed bodies, evidently beings of a different
> race and kind to anything we have seen yet.
>
> *Natal Mercury*, 1860

Finally they discovered that their marriages, Hindu and
Muslim, were not recognised by the state (so that their children
were in effect illegitimate and could not inherit from their
fathers).

Yet they confronted, adapted and won in various situations
where their cultures conflicted with those of Europe. By preventing children being born into indentureship, they resisted

the continued oppression of Indians. In 1901 (without modern contraceptives) it was reported in Mauritius that 'a female population of 116,781 Indians gave birth to a total of 9,095 babies in that year, of whom 768 were stillborn' (Hugh Tinker, *A New System of Slavery*, Oxford University Press, 1974). Indian women practised abortion throughout the period of indenture. Concern was expressed that of every one hundred Indian women who became pregnant, sixty gave birth to a stillborn child or aborted early in pregnancy. It appears to have been taken for granted that babies were strangled at birth.

These severe methods of controlling the birth rate were compounded by the high rate of suicides amongst the Indian labourers. The result was that only a small number of indentured Indians left surviving children.

The practice of birth control, as well as the high suicide rate, further diminished the family structures that in India would have been extended and socially supportive. It was through marriage, often outside the caste, religion and language, and only over several generations, that the extended family reasserted itself, and Indians recovered and re-established their social and moral structures.

South African Indians like myself have lost mother tongue, family name, religion, culture, history, and historical links with India. Cut off from India, apartheid has further separated us from the other communities in South Africa, thereby exacerbating our isolation.

The situation confronting migrants in South Africa a century ago confronts us as migrants in Europe today: we have to cope with the fact of our children losing the sense of their historical identity. Conscious that mother tongue, tradition, culture and religion could be lost in exile, migrant women attempt a balancing act between new and old countries, cultures, religions and languages. As women whose mother tongue is not English, we have a responsibility to our ancestors to preserve the language they brought into being. Should mother tongue be discarded, if we choose to live in Europe? The most valid reason for keeping a language alive is that a language develops over centuries and so gives the people who use it the strongest link with their ancestors. But if we are women whose ancestors were colonised, we may subsequently have lost our mother tongue. Our use of a European language expresses our loss.

Migration and exile are not new phenomena. Evidence of the human impulse to flee from areas threatening our survival or happiness abound in our major religions and in our history: Mohammed's flight from Mecca to Medina in the Holy Koran; the Mfecane scattering thousands of Africans in southern Africa; the destructive end of the ancient Indian civilisations at Mohenjo Daro and Harappa.

What is new reflects women's changed perception of themselves; it signals our independence and status as individuals in society: the post-modern woman makes the decision to migrate – in her own right.

In the past migration emphasised the chattel nature of a woman's existence. Women were that combination of 'things' that throughout history a woman migrant may have been: single, accompanying her parents; with a man in marriage or with the intention to marry; economically dependent wife or daughter taken from a village and transported to a city or vice versa; speaking the language of the host or totally illiterate in even her mother tongue; migrating with an entire community from her native land to the host country; a slave; or an indentured labourer.

Today's woman may decide to migrate or to go into exile with or without dependants. If married she may refuse to accompany a man into exile, or choose not to return to her native land when the man returns. She may even emigrate without her husband. Today's woman migrant may follow a profession, be skilled, and have her own capital. She may travel to a new country as an employee of a company, with a voluntary organisation, for her own or a foreign government and then decide to remain where she is employed.

It seems appropriate for the theme of this collection to be expressed in the following quotation from the Book of Ruth. I have often wondered, are Ruth's words murmured in the ear of every girl child at birth? For I can find no other way to explain the way women throughout history act out Ruth's specific commitment to follow someone to a foreign country. Expressing her commitment whilst voicing uncertainty about a new place, people and religion, Ruth, the epitome of the migrant wife, is still willing to adapt.

> Entreat me not to leave thee, or to return from following after
> thee: for whither thou goest, I will go; and where thou lodgest
> I will lodge: thy people shall be my people, and thy God my
> God.

Ruth 1. 16

High Heels

I'm playing cricket in the street with boys when Lindi comes hobbling on the pavement towards me. She's wearing high heel shoes too big for her.

Lindi poses on the pavement with her hand on her hip, pushing her hip out like she's carrying a baby. Only she got no baby. She only got a big black handbag hanging on her arm. After a bit, she changes the bag round and poses with her other hip sticking out. All the time she's tossing her head about, looking to the boys, her eyes wide like she's surprised. Only they're busy playing cricket. They're not bothered about Lindi's high heel shoes.

After a bit she yells at me, 'Hey Ruthie! What ya doing?' She throws her head my way, then looks to the boys again.

All the time I'm making like my eyes are shut, but I'm looking down at Lindi's high heel shoes. They're bright red with peep toes and shiny buckles. When I can't stand to look at Lindi's shoes any more I open my eyes wide, like I'm also surprised, and say, 'Can't you see?'

'I see ya standing in the street! Where it's dangerous!' she yells back at me.

I know what she means. She means I'm *spek'en boontjies* – like when they let you play a game but you're not really playing. I stick out my tongue. She flashes her bum. She's wearing proper panties! Then she goes on posing on the pavement, sticking her arm out so her handbag swings about. I wish I could take my eyes off her shoes.

'Ya like my shoes?' She twirls round on the pavement.

'Sissie gave it me.'

'You don't walk right in high heel shoes,' I say. But I really want to say I wish I had a sister to give me her high heel shoes.

'Ya want to try 'em on?'

I'm on the pavement before Lindi closes her mouth. She jumps back. Then she stares down at my feet like she just thought of something.

'We the same size,' I say, forgetting the shoes are too big for both of us.

Then suddenly Lindi screams out loud so everyone in the street can hear, 'Ya feet are dirty!' and hobbles away, with her handbag swinging by her side.

'Lin-di-we!' I scream after her like she left me in a burning house. 'Lin-di-we! Come back here! My feet are clean! Lin-di-we!'

But she just sways down the street away from me, on her high heel shoes, like she don't hear me. So I shout after her, 'I *wish* you fall flat on your face,' and I shut my eyes tight and scream, 'I wish! I wish!' Only she don't fall.

I'm really playing cricket in the street with the boys. I'm scouting at the top end. Say the ball comes too far behind the wicket, I must run and give it back to them. When I throw they don't get it.

Always I like to play bouncing ball when I get the ball. Till they chase me. Then I hide the ball inside my underpants and sing, 'First say when's *my* turn to bat!' When they all shout together, 'You're last man!' Only then I take the ball out, making sure they don't see I'm wearing Mattie's underpants, and toss it back to them.

Mostly I'm first man. Sometimes I'm first man and last man, if I cry when I'm out. Like today. Only now I'm getting tired waiting for the ball. I don't know how many runs the batsman got. I don't even know what number's batting. And I want to look at Hama's high heel shoes. I'm going in.

'Hey Ruthie! The game's not over.'

'I need a wee!' I say, squeezing my legs together.

Because I forget to go to the lav when I play outside they get into trouble if they don't remind me. So they shout, 'All right! All right! But make quick!'

I run inside.

Sh! Sh! Sh! The house is secret when they're outside. So full of sun. Like fairies dancing on the floor. The floorboards smell of new polish. Their door creaks. The planes swoop down at me. The net curtain huffs and puffs. Funny! I still don't reach the planes. Even standing on their beds. And I got a birthday coming.

Say you pull the bottom drawer out – Sh! – Like baby's sleeping – you can stand on it. Their things aren't for girls. You know you mustn't touch. Just look. Poor grasshopper still can't get out. Worms still in a tangle. Marbles – ugh! – still too heavy. Coca-Cola bottle tops make a jingling sound if you shake them. I never saw this plane before. It feels too soft. It mustn't be wood. Oh-oh! Better go.

I shut the door – Sh! – and turn round in the passage. The curtain moved.

I see it for the first time. There's a door behind the curtain at the end of the passage. I never knew there's a door behind the curtain. And Hama's sandals are by the door. I knock and listen. 'Hama? . . . Hama?' It's quiet. Like someone's waiting for me to go away. I try the handle. It's locked.

I do a wee and come out.

The door's still there. I rattle the handle. It's still locked. I run outside to tell the boys. 'Hey! Come and look! I found a door! I found a door.' They're not bothered about a door. They want me to scout again. Oh-oh. Lindi's coming back from the shops.

'We also got a secret door,' she says.

'You never told me about no secret door before!' I say.

'Don't get cross 'cause I c'n keep a secret.'

'You know what's behind the door?' I ask.

She looks at me down her nose and says, 'Yeah! Don't look so surprised, Ruthie! Ya not smart like me.'

'Go on, then. You can tell me now. It's no secret no more.' Lindi frowns for a bit, then she asks, 'Why *they* don't tell ya?' looking to the boys.

'Because I only just found the door, this minute!'

'Even so, betcha they don't tell ya.'

'Why?'

She laughs. 'Ya have to open it yerself.'

'But why?'

'What good's a door if ya don't open it?'

'Anyone can open a door!'

'I betcha anything, ya won't go through the door.'

'Anything?'

'Yeah!'

'*Any*-thing?'

'I said anything, baby girl.'

'Okay! I bet you your shoes.'

'I just got given these shoes!'

'You said anything, Lindi!'

'I got a handbag. Better than *this* one.'

'I don't want a handbag.'

'All right then! But . . . ya only got till . . . till yer birthday party. Then the bet's off!'

'Why?'

' 'Cause I'm invited to yer party, ain't I?'

'And so?'

'Well then, . . . ya have until yer party to go through the secret door.'

'But why?'

'Then I c'n give ya the shoes for a present, silly baby girl. Else my Ma will buy ya a present, and ya won't get high heel shoes.'

I don't understand this Lindi. But I don't want to show she's smarter than me. So I ask Mattie how many days to my birthday. My birthday's on Sunday. It's Thursday today. Mattie says that makes three days. There's plenty of time. And it's easy-peasy. All I got to do is ask Hama to unlock the secret door.

II

I wait for Hama to come through the secret door. After a bit I'm tired of waiting and maybe Hama won't ever come back, so I look for the key. I look in Hama's apron hanging on the hook. In all the tins and jars on the kitchen dresser. In the pockets of Hama's jersey and in her coat . . . Under Hama's pillow. In her handbag. I look everywhere. Even under Hama's bed. And in her shoes.

These shoes fit me – if you don't look behind. I can put my elbows on Hama's dressing table standing on the floor in high heel shoes. There's Hama's treasure. No-one must touch Hama's things. I won't touch! It's all blue glass. Children mustn't touch glass. There's a tray, two candlesticks, a powder bowl, a trinket box, a scent bottle.

Say you lift the glass lid with two hands and move your hands to the side – and bring it down slow-ly – it don't break. It's easy as pie. Hama's jewels are all colours. I can just stand and look at them all day.

I know how to put a string of pearls over my head. Only the knot won't stay. Clip-on earrings are easy. Gold bangles slip off. Hama's new lipstick tastes like apricot jam. It gets on your teeth say you press too hard. Oh-oh – crayons don't break so easy. Rouge is hard. Like a paint box. You can make it wet – with scent – or – you can scrape it with your fingernails. Like so . . . Powder don't stay in the bowl. It likes to fly around the room. And make you sneeze. Say I comb my hair, I look just like Hama. I can walk in Hama's shoes. Better than Lindi. And gold bangles don't slip off if you hold your hands up.

I go outside and stand on the stoep. The boys are still playing cricket.

'Hey Ruthie! C'mon scout for us.'

'*I'm* not Ruthie! Can't you see? I'm Hama!'

They look at me and laugh. 'Minnie Mouse! Minnie Mouse! Ruthie looks like Minnie Mouse.'

'Ba-daah!' They smash a window. Everyone's running away. Now I got the bat I'll be first man when they start again.

I shout to them, 'No need to hide! No need to hide! Hama's gone through the door! She's not coming back.'

But the whole street heard the window go, 'ba-daah!'

Everybody's coming out. Hama's come back through the door. She's standing on the stoep. I'm standing with the bat, but everyone knows it's not me made the window go 'ba-daah!'

Hama's calling 'Matthew . . . Mark . . . Paul . . . Tho-maas! Come for prayers!' They don't come. Hama calls again. 'Matthew . . . Mark . . . Paul . . . Tho-maas!'

They come out from their hiding places. One by one. I call to them, 'Cock-roa-ches! Cock-roa-ches!' They look cross with me.

'I never told Hama where you hiding! I can keep a secret!'

Then Hama sees me. She says, 'This child!' and she comes over and slaps me. She takes her jewels and shoes away. I'm left standing in the street with no shoes when Lindi comes hobbling on the pavement in her high heel shoes again. If I try to run inside she'll see I'm crying. So I turn the other way. Lucky for me Mark picks me up and says, 'Come in for the litany of the saints!' and carries me high on his shoulder where Lindi can't see my face.

The boys kneel in the front room with Hama. Only I can't keep my eyes closed. They pull faces at me when Hama isn't looking. I tiptoe outside. Now the curtain's moved back. I move the curtain and see the door still there. I come back into the front room and whisper to Hama, 'What's behind the secret door?' She puts her finger to her lips, 'Sshh!'

They finish prayers and we sit around the kitchen table. I ask everyone what's behind the door. Hama says there's nothing behind the door. Dada laughs and shakes his head.

We're having supper when Father O'Malley comes in. Father O'Malley looks around the table and says he expects one of us to be a priest. Hama quickly makes a sign of the cross.

'Hama, we already said grace,' I say.

Dada coughs.

When I ask Father O'Malley what's behind the curtain, Dada tells me to sshh! Hama says there's nothing there and Mark takes me quickly from the table.

'I'm still eating!' I say.

'Father O'Malley wants some of your food,' Mark says.

Before I go to bed I try the handle of the door. It's still locked. When I'm in bed Paul sits by me. Paul says behind the secret door is a dark, dark room. In the dark, dark room is a dark, dark bed. In the dark, dark bed is an old, old lady.

Mark comes in and says, 'Shut-up! Someone with a capital "s" will have nightmares.' They begin to whisper. Then they quarrel. They say it's a cupboard. It's a lavatory. It leads to a secret tunnel.

They don't know what's behind the door. They say we'll find out when we're grown up. Only I can't wait. I can't ever walk without high heel shoes again.

I wake up late in the night. Everyone's sleeping. I tiptoe through the house. The door's locked. Hama's slippers are outside the door. And Hama isn't in her bed. 'Hama? Let me see inside the room, just once? Please Hama. I'll be a good girl.' I wait in the passage for her to come out. I wake up back in my bed.

Then on Friday Tata and Pharti come for my birthday party. I ask Tata to show me behind the door for a birthday present. Hama says, 'No!'

Tata says to Hama, 'Let her see the room, Ma. Sunday's her birthday.'

'She'll tell Father O'Malley.'

Tata says, 'It might do him good.'

Now I know Hama won't give me the key. And I can't give up looking for it. Suddenly Hama's scent is all over the dressing table. I wipe it up with the powder puff. And Hama's standing at the bedroom door. She says I won't get a present for my birthday. But I don't want Hama's present. Hama won't give me her high heel shoes.

Now Hama's arranging flowers and polishing the candlesticks on the altar at church. I'm playing five-stones on the paving in the aisle. Hama doesn't want to leave me at home.

I hear Hama talking. But there's only me in the church. I stop playing to ask Hama who she's talking to. Hama says she's scolding God for not looking after us in a strange country.

She puts out her arms to me. When she's holding me she cries. I think hard what to say to stop her crying, so I say, 'Hama, show me what's in the room.'

She says, 'Shoo! Go play!'

III

It's Saturday. I still haven't found the key. In the morning we go to a wedding with Tata and Pharti. I sit near the front and see the bridegroom put a gold ring on the bride's finger. They receive Holy Communion. When we go to the bride's home he fastens a Tali round her neck before Father O'Malley arrives. They bathe the bride in turmeric. Then they give her a glass of milk with sliced bananas before breakfast. No-one knows what's a Tali. Even Father O'Malley doesn't know.

We come home from the wedding and Lindi calls round to tell me her Ma has gone to town to buy my present. I jump up and down on the stoep shouting, 'I don't want a present! I don't want a present! I want high heel shoes!'

'But today's Saturday. If Ma don't buy ya present today – what ya gonna do tomorrow? Ya won't have high heel shoes or a present.'

'You said the bet's on till my birthday. And my birthday's only tomorrow.'

She runs away shouting, 'Give up, Ruthie! Give up! Give up Ruthie! Give up!'

I run into the house and pull all Hama's clothes out of the dressing table drawer. I throw the pillows on the floor. I feel in the powder bowl. I empty the trinket box on the bed. The necklace breaks. The pearls roll all over the floor. I crawl about on the floor to pick up the pearls quickly before someone comes. Hama and Tata are standing at the door. I have the trinket box in my hands. And the pearls are still on the floor.

I'm not getting a present from Hama. Lindi's Ma bought me a present I don't want. And I'm not even having a birthday party.

Tata is helping me pick up the pearls while I'm crying, Hama is folding away her clothes saying, 'No birthday party!' and Tata reminds Hama about the time she pulled the dressing table cloth and pulled everything down with it. Everything broke, Tata says, but Hama says that was an accident. But I keep thinking I don't want a birthday party. No-one coming to my party will bring a pair of high heel shoes for me.

When the pearls are in the trinket box Tata fluffs up the pillows, he takes my hand and walks with me to the corner shop. We buy a chocolate cake and a bottle of Oros and a box of strawberry ice cream. At home Tata is setting one half of the table, placing a cushion on a chair for me, putting a tea towel over his arm and pretending he is a waiter serving me. Halfway through our party no-one has come to bring me a present and tears are still running down my cheeks and into my mouth, spoiling the taste of the ice cream.

So Tata takes my hand and leads me into the passage. Without even asking Hama, Tata moves the curtain. He reaches up above the door and finds the key. Tata unlocks the door, he removes his shoes, then he removes mine. I turn the handle and we go through the secret door.

I've gone through the door. It's a room. There's no sick lady anywhere. Just rugs all around the floor. Blue and black and cream and green and brown. There's a brown wooden box in the middle of the room. It's covered with flowers and leaves made of the same wood. On the box is a little oil lamp with a red chimney and little trays and vases made of brass and gold and silver. Tata lifts the red glass chimney from the lamp. He strikes a match. A yellow flame leaps up. He lights the lamp. Then he touches an orange stone. It has two hollows. Tata takes a handful of grey powder from one hollow and places it in the other. Then he strikes another match. Again a yellow flame leaps up. He puts the flame to the powder. Blue smoke curls up into the room.

Tata says, '*Saamberani*.'

The room begins to smell of strange flowers. Then Tata sits cross-legged on a red cushion. He taps the cushion next to him. I kneel on the cushion looking up at him. He joins his hands and he begins to sing softly. I can't understand what he says. I can only make out the word 'Hama'. But I like his singing. It's not like the singing in church.

I look around the room. In one corner is a picture of Jesus with a bleeding heart and a statue of his Hama. I leave the room quietly and run to tell Lindi I went through the door.

Lindi knows. She's been waiting at the front door and sees me coming through the secret door.

'But do ya know what's the secret?' she asks.

I think hard. 'It's a prayer room!'

'What's secret 'bout a prayer room?' she asks.

'I know! It's a secret prayer room!'

She claps her hands. 'Ya don't know, Ruthie. Ya don't know the secret! Ya can't have my high heel shoes.'

'Lin-di!' I scream at her. 'I went through the secret door. I won the bet.'

'What's a use of gwain through the door, if ya don't know the secret?'

Lindi and I are about to scrap when Father O'Malley arrives and I rush to show him the secret room. With his hand in mine, I pull him down the passage. Suddenly Lindi calls sharply to me. She runs down the passage, grabs my hand and pulls me back to the front door.

'Ruthie, think hard 'bout the secret and ya c'n have my shoes. Only – ya must know why it's a secret.'

So I sit down on the edge of the pavement with Lindi's high heel shoes just by my face and think real hard. What other secret is there? There must be another secret or why did no-one want to tell me what was in the room? I've gone through the door and I can't even tell Lindi the secret. Hama needn't be afraid I'll tell Father O'Malley. I don't even know what to tell. I only know there's a secret prayer room in our house. And then I remember that Hama wants the secret to be kept from Father O'Malley.

'Father O'Malley mustn't know about the prayer room,' I whisper in Lindi's ear.

When I look at Lindi's face, she's gone all sulky. Without speaking she sits next to me on the pavement and pulls off her shoes. I take off my shoes, brush the soles of my feet and put out my hand for the high heel shoes when Lindi has another idea.

'Why?' she asks. 'Ya must know why. Why mustn't Father O'Malley know?'

I still don't know. I still don't know why Father O'Malley mustn't know. I drop my hand and start to cry.

'Ya not smart like me, Ruthie. Your Hama is a Christian and that's a Hindu prayer room, silly baby girl!'

And Lindi gives me her high heel shoes. I put on the high heels and I can see Lindi wants to cry.

Then Lindi says, her face all sulky, 'If ya smart like me . . . ya'll tell me . . . I c'n have the present . . . my Ma bought for ya.'

I know I'm not smart like Lindi or why didn't I think of that?

While I stand up in my own high heel shoes, Lindi's running barefoot down the street to get my present from her Ma.

Jesus is Indian

(Who invented school? Who said little children must sit still in a desk pretending they wide awake when they dreaming of comics and swings and stealing fruit from Mrs Mumble?)

(Me, I'm not a good girl, but I'm even praying for the bell to ring, frighten even to look at Sonnyboy standing behind Sister, moving every way Sister moves and making monkey faces behind her back. You know me, once I start to laugh, I won't never stop.)

(You can't blame Sonnyboy. It's Sister's veil and skirt and things. It makes so Sister can't see what's going on right behind her. Jesus, Mary and Joseph, every time Sister look like she's turning round, I think I'm going to faint. Won't we all be in big trouble if Sister catch him? Of course yes. Even when we sitting still!)

(Here's Sister turning around – and easy as you like. Sonnyboy make like he's picking up his pencil. Poor Sister's puffed out. And she's not finished cleaning the board. Anyone can see Sister's new. Our old teacher make each one have a turn cleaning the board.)

(Now Sister's saying, No copying from the blackboard. I got to ask her why.)

'Sister, why lately Sister keep saying, No copying from the blackboard today?'

(Sister says she wants we must write from up here – she's tapping her head.)

'Then why Sister keep on changing every word we write?'

(Sister says she wants we must write like she writes.)

'But why?'

(Sister don't want me must ask so many questions.)

(The way Sister wipe the board you think she's waving to a train to stop and there's someone lying on the train lines! Now look at us! We all look like we got dandruff. And just hear how Cissie's coughing! But you know it's Cissie's own fault. Why she want to sit right under Sister's nose? Like she never talk in class and make jokes. Goody-gum-drops!)

(Before Sister turn round again I better make like I'm working hard. Maybe she'll go worry someone else. I know a good trick from last year. You fall over your desk like you sleeping and put your head on your arm so no-one can see your page, like when you doing a test and no-one must copy off you, then the teacher thinks you working hard. I just got to hide my one line of story or Sister will know I been playing. From up here in my head is coming a story about Honey.)

Me an Honey fight like tigers . . .

(Here's Sister like a ghost by my elbow. She says she wants to read my story so far. She got her red pen out.)

'Honey and I, Angelina! . . .'

'Yes, Sister.'

(Hama always say you got to respect the nuns. Because they don't get married. But Hama don't say why they don't get married. Sister's standing by Edie now. She's a good girl. She don't swear. And she don't talk back to Sister.)

Honey and I fight like tigers. Scratching. Biting. Spitting. Kicking. Pinching. Pulling hair. Hama tie . . .

(Sister's back!)

'Mother tied, Angelina! . . .'

'Yes, Sister.'

. . . Hama tied Honey and I's arms together . . .

'Mother tied our arms, Angelina! . . .'

'Yes, Sister.'

. . . Hama tied our arms together. Me an Honey pinch with the other hand . . .

'We pinch each other with our free hands, Angelina!'

'Yes, Sister.'

We pinch each other with our free hands. We scream. Like tokoloshe bite us . . .

'*Tokloshe?*'

'Don't Sister even know what's a tokoloshe? It's like a . . . like a little . . . something people can't see . . . It comes in the night . . .

like a spook . . . to bite little children.'

'As if a vampire bat bit us, Angelina! . . .'

'Yes, Sister.'

. . . as if a . . .

'Vampire . . . Angelina . . . v-a-m-p-i-r-e.'

. . .bit us. Then Hama tie. . .

'Then mother tied, Angelina! . . .'

'Yes, Sister.'

. . . Hama tied me an Honey's arms to the table leg . . .

'Then mother tied our arms, Angelina! . . .'

'Yes, Sister.'

. . . Hama tied our arms to the table leg, arms touching . . .

'. . . with our arms touching . . .'

'Yes, Sister.'

. . . with our arms touching. Hama say . . .

'Mother says, Angelina! . . .'

'Yes, Sister.'

. . . Hama says it's a sin for sisters to fight! What Hama know? Hama think Honey's so sweet . . .

'What does mother know? Mother thinks Honey is so sweet. You are a very stubborn child, Angelina . . .'

(Sister's floating away like a ghost. You can only hear the beads. I wait till she's at the far end of the class.)

'Sister, are people vampires when the we drink the body and blood on Sunday?'

(I got to hold my mouth with my two hands so I don't burst out laughing the way Sister shouting me for being cheeky.)

(This Sister Bonaventura! She make me so sick and tired I ever hear this word school! I never say I want to come to school. Why I'm wasting my time? . . . Sitting here? . . . Writing a story? . . . When my poor Hama can't even read English? And everytime I do a clean page – with neat handwriting – and no crossing out – this Sister come and spoil it with red marks! All over my clean page! Mother says this – and mother says that!)

(Edie's whispering behind her hand to me, Sh! Sister got powerful ears.)

(I'm looking at Sister's back like I can shoot poison arrows into her. Lucky for me Sister's looking somewhere else.)

Hama forget Honey and me under the table. Me an Honey fall asleep. We wake up good friends. Hapa say, no wind can blow between too-good-

to-be-true friends like me and Honey.

Even when we fight in the week, Honey and me become best of friends every Saturday. Saturday's the day we go to town alone.

Alone? The busybodies put their hands to their mouths – open their eyes wide – talking behind their hands. Me and Honey don't take notice. We got no money. But we come home an tell Hama what dresses we see. Hama cut. And Hama sew. Then Hama fit. Hama put pins in us. But me and Honey don't even say, 'Ouch!' Just in case Hama stop sewing. We say, It don't hurt, Hama. So we get ragamuffin sleeves. Sweetheart necklines. Peter Pan collars. Then we showing off. Swaying our hips with new dresses not bought from town.

One Saturday me and Honey coming from town, we see a boy standing outside his father's shop. Just a ordinary boy. Short hair cut. No moustache. All the Indian boys we know wear moustaches. So this one looks handsome. Honey and me know him. Only we never talk to him. On Sundays he bring his Hama to visit our Hama. Only he has to sit in the car and we must stay in the house. I say to this boy, 'Hello! You look busy'. Honey say I'm forward. The boy get shy because Honey standing far away like he got yellow fever. Then Honey start to walk away and I must run after her or the busybodies think he's my boyfriend.

Honey say she will tell Hama. Even Hapa. I say, what you will tell, Honey? I never stand and kiss the boy! Ooh! Honey's so shocked! She make like I commit mortal sin just to say this word 'kiss'. I say why you don't come in the shop? She say she will come in next time, if he's not my boyfriend. But he is my boyfriend, Honey. He can't be a girlfriend. Honey say I don't know what's a boyfriend.

Next Saturday Honey says she'll bring a book for the boy to read. But first we got a haircut.

From the day me and Honey can talk we begging Hama to cut our hair. I don't know why Hama must ask the big people what to do. They say Indian girls must keep hair long. Me and Honey ask, Why? Why Indian girls must keep hair long like a monkey's tail? First the big people say little girls must listen to their elders. Then when Honey and me say we getting to be big girls they say, 'It's got to do with religion!' What religion Hama? We not Hindu girls. Why we must keep our hair long? Hama say electric light children ask too many questions! Long hair take too long to dry, Hama! Say there's no sun, me and Honey can't wash our hair. Hama can see we right, but Hama say the big people will say we got no respect. Lucky for us Honey get headaches. When Hama take her to the doctor, guess what he say? He say Honey's hair is too heavy for her head! He tell Hama to cut

Honey's hair. I don't get headaches, but I cry like someone in the family just died the whole time Hama cut Honey's hair till Hama say I bring bad luck. So Hama cut my hair too.

Every busybody's shocked! Shame! Such beautiful hair! Behind Hama's back they saying, 'These Christian girls! They got no shame!' But Honey and me, we showing off. In front of all those one-plait Indian girls. Swinging our heads. Page boy hair style. Like Veronica Lake.

'Angie! Here Sister's coming again,' Edie's warning me.

(Sister's standing a long time behind my desk reading my story.)

(Sister says to leave out words that are not English.)

'Why Sister?'

'Because I don't know them, Angelina.'

'I can teach you Sister. Is easy.'

(Sister's whispering to me just like we do when we're not supposed to talk in class. Then there she goes gliding away.)

'What she say?' Edie asks.

'Sister say she never come to learn. She come to teach!'

(This Sister Bonaventura! Walking with her nose in the air! One day the rain will fall in.)

Now every Saturday Honey and me come from town, we go to the boy's shop. His shop's not busy. Me and Honey just stand and chat to him about what's showing at the bioscope. He gives us free Coca-Cola.

One night we looking in the long mirror and Honey say she's taller than me. I say, 'It's your hair Honey. Standing like a bush on top. And don't stand on your toes.' But Honey turn sideways and pull her stomach in and stick her chest out. 'You look like them pigeons in the park, Honey. Why you stand like that?' Honey say I'm jealous. 'Jealous of what, Honey?' She say I don't even know!

And then guess what? Hama say not to stand on the stoep at night. Not to play in the street any more. Why Hama? A drunk man coming pass? Hama say electric light children got no respect for their elders.

Hama say we mustn't talk to boys. And Hama say I must tell her if Honey get a boyfriend. We got no boyfriends, Hama. What we want to do with boyfriends? Hama must learn to trust us. We only want to go to parties. Do the Charleston! The Jitterbug! Foxtrot with Victor Sylvester. Hama says, 'No!' Honey and me can't go to no parties. Only if Hama is there. We only can go to weddings, engagements and christening parties. But why Hama? Hama want to dance too? Hama swing round and slap Honey's face. I got under the table in time. Honey's crying and asking why

Hama always hit the one near to her. Honey, why you never learn to do like I do? I always move slowly away before I answer Hama back.

From under the table I ask Hama how Honey and me will meet a husband? Honey and me won't meet a husband in church. 'You can't talk in church, Hama!' Hama want us to be nuns? Like Sister Bonaventura? 'We can't eat curry and rice in the convent, Hama! What's the use you teach us cooking? Hey, Hama?' Hama say Hama will choose a husband for us. Like Hapa.

But Hapa drink too much. And Hapa waste all the money for food on drink. Now Hama's trying to hit me under the table with the feather duster. Hama say, 'Who tell you such lies?' 'Hama you say so when you fight with Hapa.' Hama say she'll take some chilli powder and wash my mouth out! Hama say electric light children know too much.

I got another question to ask Sister.

'Sister? Why Sister don't just sit down and read the paper like a real teacher?'

(I can't say all the things Sister is saying now. Only remember, Sister don't like you must ask questions.)

'Sorry Sister.'

(I'm standing in front of the class smiling at my pals and making like I'm the teacher, while Sister's going down the rows. Everybody's scared even to look at me! Now I won't finish my story about Honey. Why this Sister can't leave me alone to do my writing? Why she must get cross when a person ask a simple question? Good job the bell's ringing. Everyone's running round the class putting things away.)

(Sister wants me must finish my story for homework.)

'Yes Sister.'

(Writing at home is better. There's no stopping every five minutes for Sister's red pen. And you can listen to the wireless same time.)

Suddenly Honey's putting on high heel shoes. I run to tell Hama. Hama say it's all right. But no talking to boys! 'Can I put high heel shoes on, Hama?' 'Why not? What about lipstick then, Hama?' Hama just favour Honey. Hama want Honey must get a husband and I must stay at home till I'm a old maid.

Now Honey don't want me to come in the bathroom with her. Even when she's not having a bath. Why Honey? We always bath together. Why you special, suddenly? Honey say she's a young girl. 'I'm also a young girl, Honey. How can I be a old lady?' Honey's laughing at me.

On Sunday when Hama's washing the rice and I'm stamping garlic and ginger I ask Hama, 'Why we didn't stay in India, Hama? Why Hama want us to speak our language, but Sister Bonaventura want I must leave out Indian words?' Now Hama say she don't want us to go to school anymore. Hama thought Sister Bonaventura is teaching us our language.

(I don't like this Sister Bonaventura, but I rather go to school than stay at home and do cooking and housework with Hama. Now I'm sorry I told Hama about Sister teaching us English in school.)

'You want no-one must understand us when we want to make friends, Hama? Hama! Ouch Hama!' Hama still want to beat us? But we growing big now! I leave the stamper and stand by the kitchen door, ready to run into the yard. Hama will beat us when we are big married women? Hama says, 'Yes.' And if we don't get married? Hama says she will beat us harder! But Hapa never beat Honey and me! 'I'll run away from home, Hama.' Hama say she will catch me when I come in for supper.

Now guess what? Honey say I mustn't come with her to the boy's shop any more. 'Why Honey? He's my boyfriend too. He's not only your boyfriend!'

Honey say I don't know what's a boyfriend! 'What then? What's a boyfriend? What a boyfriend do? Don't laugh Honey, don't laugh! Sister say my English better than yours. What a boyfriend do? Kiss? He kiss you? When? Why I never see?'

Never mind. I won't go with Honey if she don't want me. If Hama and Hapa find out, Honey don't blame me! I got no friends now. Hama's not worried about me, only Honey. Honey don't like me. And the boy don't like me too. Maybe I'll run away.

Honey got a nerve! She say I must wait for her outside the shop. Keep a look out. In case the busybodies come pass. What she doing in the shop? Just talking to the boy over the counter. Big romance! He was my boyfriend first. I don't like Honey any more.

(I never have time to finish my story at home because I have to help Hama in the kitchen. Sister's checking our homework. It's my turn. I close my eyes and say my prayers. All of a sudden Sister shut my book and throw it into a corner of the room.)

(Sister say, 'This is a very bad story about a very bad girl.')
'Sister?'
(Sister say I heard her.)
'I was praying Sister, I never heard you.'

(Sister ask why I never tell Hama Honey was meeting a boyfriend.)

'He's not Honey's boyfriend, Sister. He's my boyfriend. I saw him first.'

'Angelina!'

'Sister?'

(Sister's banging her flat hand on the table. She look really mad. I look at my friends in the class. Then I go to stand outside the classroom. Sister comes out. There's Sister marching away to the office. And I'm trying to catch her.)

(Sister want to write a note to Hama. She ask what's my mother's name.)

I say, 'Kamatchee.'

Sister ask, 'What's your mother's Christian name?'

'Hama got no other name Sister. Only Kamatchee, Sister.'

Sister make like she don't hear me. She ask again, 'What's your mother's Christian name?'

'Kamatchee, Sister.'

Sister's laughing. She say, 'Little Cabbage? Little Cabbage? Your mother's name is Little Cabbage?'

'No, Sister. Hama's name is Kamatchee.'

(Sister say she will write a note to Little Cabbage if I don't tell her Hama's Christian name.)

'Sister Bonaventura, why you can't learn to say Hama's name? Why you say "Little Cabbage", "Little Cabbage", "Little Cabbage"? Hama's name is Kamatchee. Say Kamatchee. Go on, Sister. Say "Ka-ma-chee".'

(Ooh! The way Sister's going on. Like the Sermon on the Mount.)

'Sorry Sister. Hama never told me is a sin for a Christian to have a Hindu name.'

(Jesus, Mary and Joseph, rather send me a book for Christmas with all the Christian names so I don't give my children a Hindu name by mistake. I don't want my poor children must die and go to hell for damn nation.)

(If I tell Hama Sister chased me away from school, Hama will be glad because she don't want me to learn English. Anyway, now I got time to lie in bed and I can finish my story and not worry about that Sister Bonaventura and her red pen.)

I knew it! Honey's been found out. She think she can go alone into the shop every Saturday afternoon and talk to the boy and the busybodies won't talk? Now she's going to get a hiding. The boy's in the front room. With his Hama and Hapa. Their car is parked outside. All the children in the street climbing all over the car. And Honey's hiding in the kitchen.

I told you, Honey. It's okay to speak to a boyfriend when you a good girl like me but not when Hama say you can't stand on the stoep at night.

Honey says I told Hama. I didn't! How can I do such a thing? Didn't I visit the boy too before Honey got big ideas about him? I thought Honey want to hit me, but she's standing there shivering. 'Honey I never told Hama. True as God. Must be the busybodies.'

Hama's in the kitchen with us. Hama want us to make tea. Honey don't want to take the tray inside. But I'm not frightened of the big people.

The boy's there. All dressed up. He never come in before. Always drops his mother and comes to pick her up. His Hama and Hapa are there too. All dressed up in Sunday clothes. One auntie and one uncle are smiling, smiling, smiling, all the time I pass the tea around. But Hama and Hapa look very suspicious.

Just when I want to put a cup on the side table my eyes catch a small gold tray. Looks like a nutmeg, turmeric sticks and some leaves on the tray. I look at Hama and Hapa. They don't look comfortable.

I go back to the kitchen to tell Honey what they doing. Hama comes in. Hama goes up to Honey and begins pinching Honey's cheek, like she's playing, but also like she's cross. 'What you been up to, hey?' Honey says, 'Nothing Hama, nothing.' Now I'm getting scared. I say, 'It wasn't Honey's fault, Hama. It's my fault. Don't hit Honey.' I pull Honey away from Hama and try to get Honey under the table. But Honey's like she's stuck. And Hama don't stop. She keep asking Honey the same question, 'What you been up to, hey?' – till Honey burst into tears. Then I burst into tears.

Then Hama laugh. Just in time. Hama say they come to ask for Honey to marry the boy. Lucky I never tell Hama about going to the boy's shop on Saturdays.

(Jesus, Mary and Joseph, forgive me for being so selfish. Thinking about my children going to heaven and forgetting about my poor Hama. Rather don't give me that book for Christmas. Rather tell me how my poor Hama will go to heaven if she got a Hindu name? Must I give up chocolates for Lent? Or boyfriends?)

'Hama, why you didn't get a Christian name when Father baptised you?'

(Hama say if she's a Christian and her name is Kamatchee then Kamatchee is a Christian name.)

(Honestly! This Hama got a answer for everything. Maybe she should go to Sister's school. She will learn better than me.)

'But Hama, Sister say you won't go to heaven. Because you got a Hindu name.'

Hama laugh. Hama holds her head up high and makes it wobble about. She say, '*What* that sister know? Hey? Don't Jesus wear a dhoti like Gandhi? Don't Hama talk to Jesus in our language? Don't Jesus answer all Hama's prayers? Don't Honey get a rich husband? You so clever, what you think that means? Hey? You electric light children and you don't know? Jesus is Indian. You go to school and tell that Sister.'

(Jesus, Mary and Joseph, never mind what I said before about the book with Christian names. First I want to go to town to do window shopping before I tell you what to get me for Christmas.)

(Hama never get the letter from Sister, so I go to school to say I'm sorry. For three days Sister don't want me to come in the class. So I stand by the door all day. On the third day Sister say I can come inside.)

(Now Sister's come to mark my story to see if I take out the boyfriend. But I left it in. Because the boyfriend is going to marry Honey. Then Sister ask me in front of the whole class what's this Indian word doing in my English story? Every page got this Indian word two or three times even. Sister say I'm stubborn like a mule.)

(So I stand up in front of the whole class and I tell Sister I never going to call Hama 'mother'. Even when I'm writing English in my book. Sister can say mother for Sister's mother. I say Hama for my Hama. Because Hama say Jesus is Indian because Jesus wear a dhoti and Jesus can understand our language.)

(I know the busybodies going to hear about this and say I got no respect for a holy servant of God. And I'm waiting for Sister to send me home again. And then Sister say, 'All right Angelina.' And everyone is turning to look at me. And now I'm swinging my page boy haircut, and pulling in my stomach and pushing out my chest when I walk home from school.)

Poppy

The breeze felt hot. It came blowing towards them up the hill in little gusts, skimming low over the top of the wild grass so that the pointed, dried up tips appeared combed back. Each time it reached the red-petalled flower growing wild in the veld, the flower shook, its petals fluttered, with neither breeze nor petal making a sound.

The flower's knobbly, delicate stem seemed willing to compromise with the breeze in whichever direction it chose to blow. It bowed, it swayed, it strained, it stooped, But each new force of the breeze rejected the compromise. *It* swooped and swirled in continuous spirals round and round the flower, first crumpling, then stiffening, then flattening out the paper-thin petals. It seemed to her to be inviting the flower's resistance or to be taunting its lack of opposition.

One will blow away, she thought, each time a sharp burst tugged at the petals. One will blow away now that the breeze seemed to have gathered momentum from somewhere. One will surely blow away should the breeze toss the flower head wildly about once more. Yet the flower held itself intact, until the different strategies of the breeze failed and it dissipated itself arrogantly in swooping movements directed victoriously upwards to the sky.

The red flower grew still. Its petals relaxed, then slowly unfurled. At last she could see its vibrant redness vivid against the blackness at its centre. Now it looked vulnerable to her. Unsuspecting, trusting and softly vulnerable. It was as if, having contended with and resisted the wantonness of the breeze, the singularly beautiful flower could envisage no other threat to its purpose in life – to grow and produce seeds.

She was engrossed, staring abstractedly at the red-petalled flower when suddenly a greenish-white butterfuly poised within the perimeter of its cup. It was as if an invisible hand had wilfully placed it there. An unmarked butterfly, with nothing striking about it, merely a hint of green, perched fairy-like on the bristly black protuberance at the flower's centre. *It* will be carried away if the breeze returns, she thought. It will fly away should she move.

She watched while the butterfly flickered, then began a languid movement of its greenish-white wings. It was if they were mating. Plant and animal. The sensual movement of the faded wings and the bright, captive flower gripped beneath, reminding her of *Leda and the Swan*. Another incongruous mating.

And yet, while she sat motionless near the red flower, its red petals tissue-paper thin and creased were, to her, like just another colour of the finely veined green wings. The image of the two fragile beings engrossed in their compatible world disturbed her. She glanced away.

In the distance she saw the farming landscape, squares of cultivated land down the slopes of the hills, modern silvery windmills on top of metal stilts, brown-thatched rondavels and red and green corrugated farm buildings clustered together here and there in the valley. Nearer she made out the Land Rover, more from the brown-hazed dust moving in a cloud with it, than from any other recognisable sign. *It* also seeming incongruous and active in the rooted landscape. Its purposeful approach was like a reminder to them of the cultivated life below.

The farm below described a circle of welcoming homes, and generations of families farming the land; of love for the land and for seasonal growth; and of love between those who shared the experience. But she was outside that welcoming circle. When she had thought about experiencing love it had been in the unromantic sense. She knew there would be more than one man in her life, but that with one man there would remain a connecting thread that would outlast even separation. In those dreams she had pictured every description of man, but this one.

At fifteen she had never known fear: she had experienced waking up unaccountably afraid in a quiet, darkened house, listening intently for any familiar sound to reassure her – the reassurance often coming from the sound of her father coughing in his room; she had been awed into a state hovering between absolute disbelief and the suspicion of a faint possibility – that such things could happen, while listening to her uncle spinning yarns about tokoloshes throwing objects about in a room and ghosts that followed one home after midnight. But these fears depended on her imagination to frighten her and could be dispelled as easily as flicking a light switch.

And then she was sixteen, on a night train bound for the Transvaal. She was scheduled to change at Bloemfontein at six in the morning, but a couple of officials on the train stopped by her and slowly and carefully reiterated that she had, instead, to change at one o'clock in the morning at a remote station she had never heard of, and wait there until three for a train that would take her on to Bloemfontein. She was offered no alternative. She was put off on the track in the middle of the night. The signalman lighted her way across the metal lines filled in with gravel stones. She was then slightly afraid.

There were no people on the small platform. There was no-one in the waiting room. Her apprehension grew.

The signalman could see that she was afraid. He thought she might be better off travelling on to the next station which would be reached when it was growing light. He promptly stopped the next goods train in the middle of the track and once again he lighted her way across the gravel. He put her in the guard's van and shut the door. The train lurched forward.

The cabin was unlit. The light of the signalman's lamp had revealed the shapes of two benches on opposite sides of the cabin before the door had shut. The forward movement of the train propelled her towards one side. In stumbling she sat down in total darkness as the train hurtled onwards.

When she heard the noise at the door, she had been travelling for almost an hour. There was not time, however, to brush aside the noise. The door swung open letting in a blast of wind. She turned in terror to the open space. The man who stood there said simply, 'Do you mind if I sit here with you?' The door shut. The cabin was dark once more. It was then she experienced dread.

She could not see where the man was. She could neither make out if he was moving towards her or standing still. Then she heard a sagging movement on the opposite bench and the man became a solid shadow in the windowless cabin. She knew fear then.

The cabin opened directly on to the railway track. For the man to have made his way to the rear of the train where the guard's van was positioned, he must have moved along the side of the speeding train, gripping the hand rails all along the sides. The recurring image of the man moving in this manner towards the cabin where she sat, horrified her.

He had spoken in English – she had recognised the accent of an Englishman living in the north, or an Afrikaner living in the south.

Other than that he could have been anyone – the guard, the signalman, or anyone else for that matter. The question he had asked before stepping into the cabin was all he had said. Now he said nothing to her and, oddly, her fears did not grow less the longer they sat in silence in the dark.

The imagination that thrived on romance, heroic myths and horror stories, was like a nonentity in this experience of fear. They were in South Africa. She was black. The man was white. There was nothing else for the imagination to build on – there was nothing to see of the man. This was the kind of fear from which she could not get up and run away. It was the kind of fear from which no-one could rescue her. And the cabin remained totally dark. She was afraid to speak to the man and she feared their silence. Without thinking, she prayed.

When the train stopped it was beginning to grow light. The man slipped out of the cabin without either of them saying a word to each other. Not a single aspect of him as a person remained with her. She refused to question the man's motive or his awareness (or lack of it) that she could have been frightened. But, whatever the direction she had been growing towards in her understanding of South Africa, it was redirected by this experience.

When she met him she was trusting. It was the quality about her that singled her out from other women. It formed the connecting thread between them. He was surprised that she was able to love him without any sense of their differences.

Now, she watched him extend a large, square-fingered hand and slowly enclose both the red-petalled flower and the greenish-white butterfly. Turning to her lying in the wild grass, he gently drew her towards him, unfurled her fingers and placed the bruised flower and the dying butterfly in her palm. She looked at the two, the red petals crushed on one, the whitish wings powdery on the other, and her face softened. With both his fair hands cupped beneath her black ones they watched the trapped movements of the hurt wings against the bruised petals.

'Like these two,' he said, 'vulnerable, sharing an act in life, we'll be crushed.'

She made rocking movements with her hands, crooning something he had no memory of, while the wings beat with diminishing vigour and the sound of the Land Rover faintly merged with their fears.

A Bag of Sweets

You would have thought the past three years had never happened, the way my sister Khadija breezed into the family shop and stood beaming at me, radiating that glow that comes from knowing someone is surprised and overjoyed to see you.

Like a good Muslim woman, her hair was tucked under a blue chiffon scarf, she wore a delicate peach lipstick – but her legs were bare. She had discarded the traditional trousers Muslim women wear with a dress.

Looking at her, standing there not attempting to hide her delight at surprising me, nor her own joy at seeing me, I marvelled at all she had forgotten.

After several minutes delighting in the joy of that meeting, her voice burst from her, as if a hand clamped over her mouth the past three years had just been removed. 'Kal-toum!' she said, stepping forward to embrace me.

Without thinking, I side stepped, moving out of her reach. She knew I was never any good at pretending to be civil or courteous. Social niceties were never important to me. Khadija knew that. Safely behind the counter I made a pretext of flipping idly through a magazine, the way I would have done if there was no-one in the shop with me.

I have to say this for Khadija, she was blessed with humility. She stepped up to the counter, folded her arms across the top, and began speaking spontaneously about how wonderful a man her husband was, how beautiful their baby looked, how homesick she was for our New Year's picnic at the beach, how she missed the things we took for granted, and how she missed me more than anyone else. It failed to move me.

I felt as cold towards her as the last kiss I gave to anyone.

Her hands resting easily on the cold glass counter were like a bird's wings, relaxed, yet with the potential for unimaginable flight. I could see those hands running across the keyboard, typing, playing the piano. Those hands had given her freedom. In doing so they destroyed the people we loved.

These feelings Khadija seemed not to share. She was insensible to the hurt I felt. She rambled on. The details of what she said I do not even recall. I was determined to meet her lack of sensitivity with a show of disinterest. Out of boredom I repeatedly glanced at my watch. This did not ruffle her. Finally I turned my back on her and began weighing out bags of sugar.

Our shop was small. There was one door, just one glass display case and standing all round the floor space were sacks of rice, sugar and flour, propped up against drums of spices.

Without asking, Khadija came around the counter and began to help me, still talking without interruption.

I could not tolerate the natural way she did this; as if she still belonged with us; as if she had done nothing to hurt us; as if her bid for freedom had not destroyed our family.

So I pushed her away. I pushed her away, without malice, without calculation, without thought of the consequences. It was like a spontaneous movement to brush aside the horror of one's other self.

It was as I pushed her violently away and she reached out to stop herself falling, that I noticed how much she resembled our dead mother. For a second I thought it was my mother I had struck.

Khadija had finally stopped speaking. She was looking at me with a kind of waiting apprehension on her face, as if she expected me to follow through with a slap to the face. But the shock of seeing the resemblance unnerved me. We only stared at each other. She had no way of knowing what I was thinking.

I expected her, then, to draw herself up and walk out of the shop . . . perhaps forever . . . the way she had walked out of our home three years ago. But three years ago there was no cause for pride. Three years ago I had wanted her to go, for the disgrace she was bringing to our family. Yet I begged her not to go, thinking we could avert the gossip and shame. But now, I did not want her to go. I wanted to stand looking at her face, noting the eyes, the brow, the mouth that was so much like our mother's.

And it seemed ironic that of all of us, she should be the one to remind me of our mother.

Instead of saying that to her, instead of reaching out to hold her, of sharing my grief with her, I reached up and pulled down the blinds in the windows, switched off the lights and moved to the door with the keys in my hand.

Love is a funny thing. Khadija, her face softened, smiling and vulnerable, said, 'I'll visit you again, Kaltoum,' then she left.

Over the past year she had been calling at our home daily without fail, knocking at our door, waiting like a stranger for someone to answer, smiling sweetly at whoever opened the door, asking if she could visit us – now. Now our parents were dead. Just the way a stranger would have done. And throughout that year we had quietly shut the door in her face. As if we were strangers. Each of us, her brothers and sisters.

It was the most natural thing we ever did. The family had not discussed any plan of action. Each of us, when faced with Khadija standing at the door, felt we could do no more than shut it in her face. It was not that we could not forgive her for wanting the right to choose whom she should marry; it was the consequences of that freedom we could not forget. Our parents died within months of each other.

Give Khadija her due – she was an intelligent woman. It seemed a shrewd thing for her to turn from visiting our home to visiting the family shop. And to her credit she made no pretext of having come to buy anything.

The family still refused to speak to her, some of us showing more hostility than others. Undaunted, she would stand alongside the counter, chatting to whoever was on duty in the shop, taking no offence that no-one ever replied to anything she said.

Instead she conversed with herself, replying to the questions she posed and the remarks she made, and the conversation developed a style of its own.

I had been closest to her and I was now the obstacle to the rest of the family forgiving her. If I relented, Khadija must have known, the rest of the family would welcome her home, since I was the eldest. Believing this, she concentrated on visiting the family shop when I was there. This happened to be on Fridays. Our brothers were at prayer.

When I realised that she was coming regularly to the shop while I was on duty, I in turn developed my own style of defence. With meticulous attention to detail I dusted the counter; swept the floor; polished the glass case; weighed out bags of sugar, rice and flour; while she conversed out loud with herself in her light-hearted, superbly acted way.

I ignored her for varying moments of time until I reached for the window blinds, the light switch and the keys. At this stage I would lock up the shop. But one day, as if in a trance, I reached for a fistful of sweets, placed it in a paper bag and shoved it into her arms as they lay folded across the counter. Khadija stopped speaking. Her face softened. Quietly she closed her hands around the bag of sweets and left the shop.

It was several weeks before I could bring myself to tell the family. They were astonished, my brother Abdul especially.

'A bag of sweets?' they asked incredulously.

'Cheap sweets!' I replied in an off-hand way, my voice sounding flat, final, while I was cruelly delighting in the effect I was having on the others.

They questioned me, registering their disbelief.

'Yet she comes back?'

'Every Friday!' I said emphatically.

They did not know how to interpret this turn of events and I saw the beginning of a sense of wrong among some of them. Whereas before they were angry with her for what she had done three years ago and the effects of it – now they turned to criticising her for persistently coming to us when we were rejecting her, and forcing us into doing wrong.

'She shouldn't come on Fridays,' they agreed.

'That makes me really sore,' my brother said. 'She is a Muslim girl. She knows it's our custom to pray at the Mosque on Fridays.'

But Khadija was married into a Christian family that was involved in voluntary work, fasting during Lent, eating fish on Fridays and everything else Christian. My Christian friends said that on Fridays we should be more forgiving! That was why she was coming on Fridays. Abdul would not believe me. 'A bag of sweets?' he kept repeating. 'You're sure about that, Kaltoum? A bag of sweets?'

'Sure I'm sure. Cheap sweets!'

'You're pulling a fast one on me. Why a bag of sweets? Why not fruit? Or sugar? Flour? If you're weighing the stuff?'

'It's what you'd do to a child, isn't it? To get rid of it? You give it a bag of sweets.'

'She would leave in time,' he said.

I knew he would have forgiven Khadija the very day she ran away to marry the Christian boy. But he had to take his cue from our parents.

'It's like you would insult someone. Listen. You know that rich family who live in the valley? They're very generous to everyone, aren't they? But do you know what they do to someone who has spoken ill of them and then has the cheek to visit?'

He did not know. 'They dish up some food in a bowl, wrap it in a cloth, and give it to the visitor.'

'What does that mean?'

'It's to say we will not eat with you. Eating with people is a big thing with us. The visitor goes soon after.'

'I can see you want to make Khadija feel cheap! But why does she come back?'

'She doesn't take the insult. She knows I want to make her not to come back. But she wants to come back. Like a woman when she loves a man who beats her up. After each beating they make up. She forgives him. She makes excuses for why he beats her up. She says he is possessive. She says it's because he loves her but can't control his jealousy!' We sat pensively for a while.

'Perhaps it's guilt,' he whispered.

'Guilt?' I asked angrily. 'Whose guilt? My guilt? It's got nothing to do with me. I'm only a sister. It's what it did to . . .'

'With her being the youngest sister. You were close to her.'

'You think I was jealous?'

'No. But she might have told you. Instead of you finding out with all the rest. You were hurt.'

'Maybe so.'

'You must've been terribly hurt.'

I was silent.

'It isn't as if she turned Christian. She just married one.'

'It might have been better if she had,' he said.

'Turned Christian? I think turning is worse. Much worse. Think how you'd feel.'

'Poor Khadija,' he said.

'Yes. Now they don't want her and we don't want her.'

'She should've turned Christian,' he said.

'You think if she turned they will treat her any different? Christians are funny people.'

'If you throw your lot in with someone, it's no good keeping something back. She should've turned,' he said.

'No, then we could never forgive her.'

'She'll stop someday,' he said.

'Yes, one day she won't feel to come. Still, I wouldn't come Fridays.'

'I wouldn't come at all. But a bag of sweets, Kaltoum?'

'Cheap sweets!'

I can still see her face when I close my eyes, her lips softened, just for a second, before she regained control. One Friday Khadija did not come in to the shop, although I waited for her past closing time.

The Well-Loved Woman

To a child it was no bother, seeing the man standing idly, leaning against a pillar. A child just skips on by. But with approaching adolescence, having to pass him became a cause for shyness.

He was an African, appearing one day as if from out of the blue to lean against the pillar. As Chantal grew older, he greeted her. Just a nod. Hardly a movement of his head. Never a word. Recognition that she was a young woman.

Directly he began greeting her, she began to speculate about him. How had she never seen him before? When had he come? Or had he always stood there without her noticing him? Where did he disappear to at night? Why did no-one ever speak to him? And why did he stand there like that? As if he were waiting – without hope.

On Fridays he wore a round, crocheted white cap.

Without warning, she was suddenly self-conscious when there were boys around her. The very same boys she always hung about with in the playground made her feel clumsy; made her legs drag like wooden blocks, left her agonising over – not just her appearance – but how she appeared to them. Were her legs too slim? Did she look funny in the ijaar? What were the boys thinking of her?

Funny, there had always been boys in her class. She sat next to Ebie, did her homework with Dinesh and walked home from school with Ling. But somewhere on the uneventful passage between home and school, something changed. She became engrossed in really looking at boys as if she had never seen one before; watching them with the furtive fascination of a for-bidden book; noticing things about them like their lips and the fine hairs beginning to show on their upper lip; the varying shades of colour on their skins, ranging from uniform black to rich russet shades of brown, honey and gold. She observed that their hips were narrow, their shoulders wide. The way they hooked their thumbs in their belts delighted her; and she became spellbound just watching them move in stovepipe jeans. They swaggered about.

But the stranger stood still. Marked by a certain look she could not equate with anything she knew, because it was outside her experience. Yet it did not lessen the longing to name the look in his eyes, to discover how it came to be there.

Passing him one day instead of nodding in her usual quick self-conscious way, eyes on the hopscotch markings on the pavement, she glanced artlessly up into his face and straight into brown eyes that softened when they looked at her, but quickly turned away on meeting her eyes. Inexplicably she remembered the sixteenth candle on her birthday cake. The one she had not blown out, that she left burning, and melting on to the chocolate icing, while slicing all around it, until finally it glimmered weakly and snuffed itself out.

The candles on her cake were blue. The stranger was handsome. His skin deep brown like her father's. His hair tightly curled.

With the innocence of a child she asked questions about him. At first no-one knew. His surname. His age. Where he went home to at the end of the day. They claimed to know nothing about him except his habit of standing outside the place where he worked when business was slack.

When she persisted they said – hoping to place him in an unfavourable light – 'He stops working whenever a woman passes.'

'Does that mean I'm a woman?' she asked, naively picking up what they had not intended her to.

They would not give her the honour. 'You'll be a woman when a man marries you!'

'And if I never marry? Will I never be a woman?'

The idea of not marrying could not even be considered. The question should never have been asked. They admonished her with something new, 'Don't *you* go falling in love with him! He's a skelm.'

Like a child she did not think of asking who else had been in love with him. Her heart leapt up for the simple joy of knowing they knew him. While she was ignorant of why this should bring joy to her, she was certain whatever they knew of him was wrong.

'He never wolf whistles! Never makes rude remarks! Like the boys from good families. He never even smiles! He isn't standing there to ogle women! That's your idea of every man!'

Short of asking him, she could only continue to be intrigued, creating reasons for what caused the look in his eyes. She started off convinced he must have been deserted by his mother: her mother had hoped for a son, his must have hoped for a daughter. Next she thought his family disowned him for some error in his youth: she was caught holding hands with Ebie – and no-one spoke to her for a week. Then she believed he was faithful and true to his first love – who died: Dinesh had moved to Johannesburg. Finally she hit upon the idea that he was deeply hurt by a girl. She pictured him in each situation with that distant look in his eyes. Then she dreamt about what he would be like happy and in love.

She resolved to love him and he would be blissfully happy.

Two weeks after her sixteenth birthday, Ling kissed her – her first kiss – outside the school gates. Now each night in bed she created a romantic story with herself as the heroine and the stranger as hero. The details of the story varied from one night to the next: he went from disowned prince to movie star, escaped prisoner, secret agent, poet. Often a story would continue the next night. She could not wait to get to bed. They made passionate love in her dreams.

Their love making stopped at kissing.

Now whenever she passed the stranger she felt there was a secret between them. Dinesh, Ebie and Ling were too young! They did not know the meaning of love. This was love. She was in love with this strange man. Before leaving the house for school each day, she fussed over her hair, put on lipstick, eye shadow, eye liner, mascara, rubbed everything away just slightly, so the teachers would suspect but be uncertain. She was preparing to meet a lover. Passing him on her way to school she read love and adoration in his face when he nodded at her with his eyes turned away.

Out of the blue her sister, who married and left home when Chantal was ten, arrived from England, presenting her with the kind of person she had never known. It was the custom that someone returning from a spell away from home had to visit each member of the family, beginning with the eldest. Like a dutiful daughter Kamilla set about doing this, renewing old friendships, paying her respects. Chantal followed her everywhere, captivated by her sister's serenity. Seeing the two of them together, everyone remarked at how much Chantal had grown to resemble her sister.

And Chantal, for her part, sensed something unmistakable in the air wherever they went. Pleasure. A sense of good feeling. Just at seeing her sister. She was small, black-haired, vivacious with clear grey eyes. But she also sensed – why did she sense this? – something secret between Kamilla and the other women. Now the man no longer had monopoly over Chantal's sense of mystery. Kamila, too, intrigued her, exuding this air of being beloved by all in the community, yet seeming to flaunt some secret knowledge the women had about what the love was based on.

Chantal was excluded from sharing the confidence of the circle of women. She had to be content with catching snatches of conversation, hinting at this, whispers, smiling secretly at that. The sense of unknowing increased her bewilderment. After all, Kamilla was just like all the other women in the family, married with a few babies. Why this special love for her?

They lulled her curiosity, they discussed flowers, using the liquidiser to prepare time-consuming dishes, freezing traditional foods. Endlessly. They exchanged recipes, did each other's hair, made each other up to look like Indian actresses, with Chantal half-knowing it was all a cover-up. Perhaps to keep the men in the family contented. Perhaps to lull her own suspicions.

The first move out of the women's secret circle came when Kamilla announced she had come home to find someone willing to take care of her children while she went to university.

Her friends were scandalised by the idea. No married woman in the community had dared imagine such a thing. 'Leave your husband and children and go to college?' they whispered fearfully. Their show of shock delighted her. She laughed and nodded. Since her husband agreed, there was nothing anyone could do about it. Everything rested on her husband's agreement.

What Kamilla would have done had her husband disagreed, she never said. And no-one dared to ask.

Without fuss, arrangements were made for Kamilla's children to be left in the community. More than ever, Chantal sensed she was acting from a confidence that had not come only from her status as a married woman.

The young people now looked up to her. They hung around her; told her their hidden ambitions; whom they secretly loved. Kamilla pursued their interests. She suggested the unmarried girls in the family should have a chance to go to university, college, run the family business, be mechanics – whatever the goal – they should pursue it.

It created a rumpus. The women trembled to leave their daughters alone with her.

But the unrest could not last. She was not an outsider. She was amongst friends of her own age. What was more, she argued pleasingly. How could she be ostracised? She was a well-loved woman.

Her friends expressed fears that the destiny of their daughters – as wives and mothers – would be threatened.

'Our girls will despise our tradition if they're educated!' they complained. And – as if it were the final damnation – 'Men don't marry educated girls!'

'Ask yourself why?' Kamilla said.

They shrugged. 'Educated girls don't accept a man as head of the house.'

Her solution was simple. 'Educated girls must find men who don't want to be head of the house.' She said it with a laugh.

'Then they'll remain old maids! All men want to be the head of the house.'

'If a man is old fashioned, *he* shouldn't find a wife,' she said. And then she described how girls could be trained at college, in nursing schools, how they may work at night in factories, hospitals. But even she conceded that fathers would not allow their unmarried daughters to leave home or to work nights. 'Husbands might.'

'They should!' Kamilla said. 'And if they don't, our girls will run away from home.'

'But if we give our girls this freedom, and our men refuse to marry them, who will marry these girls, then?'

For days and days Kamilla would not answer. She laughed uncontrollably each time the question was put to her. She brushed aside their pleas for an explanation. She wanted them to provide the answer.

When they despaired of ever speaking the solution – they knew it – she said it for them: 'Let our girls choose their husbands. Instead of sitting at home while brave young men come forward with proposals, let our girls come home with a young man and say – this is the man I want to marry.'

Even here she was well loved. Even through the women's doubts about 'this falling in love business', her ideas did not put their backs up. And once offered to the young people, the idea was left to have its effect.

Still innocently trying to feel her way through this period of half-knowledge, Chantal began to wonder if her sister was in love? Was her marriage not arranged? How had she met her husband?

Kamilla would not say. She refused to say anything about herself.

'Then tell me, how will I know when I'm in love?' Chantal begged her.

'When you feel you want to put out your hand and touch a man,' she said.

Chantal felt a new restlessness stirring. She wanted to test the women to see if they were as liberal as they sounded. She wanted to say, I am in love with a man. May I bring him home with me? May I go to college? May I sleep the night with a friend? But she said none of these things to her family. Only to Kamilla.

Her sister said, 'When your time comes, you won't ask, you'll do the thing you want to do.'

Then the community was shattered by the news that Chantal was found speaking to the stranger who leaned against the pillar when business was slack.

'An Indian girl! Speaking with an African man!' sent shock waves through the community.

'No-one in this city will marry you now! We'll have to send for a husband from India for you!' they cried.

'I didn't do anything. I just talked to him.'

'Wicked girl! What you want with him? You can't marry him.'

'Can't an African marry an Indian?' she asked in all innocence.

Her mother slapped her face. Her brothers threatened to beat up the stranger.

'Where will you live if you marry an African?' they demanded.

She stole out of the house to put this question to the man. Her brothers beat her up.

She was forbidden to leave the house and threatened with another beating if she was found speaking to the stranger again.

In her room, crying, bruised, shocked that she had been beaten, perplexed by the anger the incident had caused, she learnt that the family bristled with suspicions of Kamilla's part in her rebellion. But her brothers could not touch the elder sister – she was a married woman. Only her husband could.

Kamilla resisted all their questions, while refusing to extricate herself from blame. She explained to Chantal the seeming contradictions all young women were facing.

'You'll be allowed to do things they wouldn't allow me to do. Because our parents are learning with us. It's always harder for the first child. Parents are hardest with the first child because they're inexperienced. If I had been found speaking with a boy – any boy – I'd be married before the week was out – to someone else. Because we love our parents, we conform to some of the things they want from us – we test them in other ways. Each of us has to judge when to conform, and what to challenge. If we find we're conforming more than we are challenging, we may have to marry to gain our freedom. Think about it. What you want to do, and are prevented from doing, you'll allow your children to do. Won't you?'

Kamilla planned her strategy. Her friends were forewarned that she would be broaching the matter of Chantal's punishment with her parents. They converged on her home eager to be present at whatever was to take place. The matter was spoken of gently, with Kamilla touching her parents hands, advising them that action could be taken against her brothers for beating Chantal. 'Unpleasant for the family, and for the community,' she said. 'After all,' she said, 'Chantal only spoke to him. She's a child. You know he's my age. Don't I know him? Don't I know he can be trusted? He is a gentleman.'

It left Chantal puzzling over how Kamilla was able to speak to the family in this way. Could it rest on the simple fact of her being well loved? Why was she more loved than others? How could she speak so intimately of an African man and not be divorced by her husband? Was it because she lived far away and they missed her?

At the end of a month, Kamilla's husband arrived to fly home with her. To Chantal they appeared deeply in love.

On her last day Kamilla went on a shopping expedition, 'Presents for all the little ones back home,' she said. With Chantal, she took her newest baby.

She talked breezily while they left the suburb and approached the town. It was as they neared the shop where the man leaned against the pillar that Chantal noticed he was not standing outside his shop.

Without a word of explanation, Kamilla walked into the shop.

He was standing watching the door as they entered. Kamilla simply walked up to him and they stood for several minutes looking at each other. Neither touched nor spoke. Then Kamilla put out her hand to touch his face. Turning to the child, then to the man, she said, 'Maqhmoud, this is my son, Maqhmoud.'

Child and Dove

It is raining softly through the night. The rain falls swiftly. Shot, like silver needles from the sky. Striking prostrate figures, on the ground. Splattering off rigid surfaces in the dark. Spilling over and across the sloping roofs. Rain falling with frenzied insistence. Water running alongside the eaves. Tumbling into drainpipes. Rushing downwards. Spurting to the ground. Swirling around stones. Eddying through the metal bars of grates. Flowing quietly in the eroded sluits. Soundlessly deepening a myriad tiny lines etched into the ground. Throughout the night. All night. A steady drizzle hovering opaquely in space.

All night crouching beneath the car. Easing her body fearfully into changing positions on the muddy ground. The machine gun patter of the rain. The choking gurgle of the water. All night. Muffling the warning stamp of men's boots. That dare her to come out.

With hunger cramping her abdomen. Cold stiffening her limbs. Hair, matted and wet, filtering out the running mud. Her school blouse like a sponge, soaking up the running water that washes away the stains of blood that is not hers. Would others dare come out? To cloak her female terror of these men?

Who were these men? Who are these others? Whose is the agonised scream she hears each time she closes her eyes?

Loosing hold of her surroundings, then coming back to the sound of rain falling softly on the wet ground. Strange music. Filtering through her conscious nightmare. The playful swirl of water. The pretty eddying circles. The wanton tumbling to another level. Fading in and out of her slackening consciousness. Fainting and waking throughout the night. All night. Trying to grasp hold of who she is. What had brought her to this fearful place? Who are they who would dare to come to her?

Abruptly the rain stops. As if a voice dictated, 'Cut!' and the frenzied, mindless activity froze into censored silence. In the betraying stillness listening confusedly to the large drops falling without inhibition to the wet ground. Each time with an amplified 'Plop!' Each time reacting as if a gun had sounded. Bruising her body in the confined space.

Then surfacing from a succession of timeless absences to find the water that had escaped along the gutter to the storm drain down the street, gathering in trembling puddles around her feet; hiding in the lifeless hollow she had shaped for her head; laying trapped by the angular curves of her young body.

Was she fainting? Or dying? No-one would find her.

Conditioned like a moth careless in its attempts to reach the light, crawling out of the wet with a crippled, sideways motion, to just within the outer edge of the abandoned car. Flakes of rusted metal catching hold of her hair as she moves; metal dust raining on to her face. From her hiding place disorientated beneath the car, she stares up at this place where she has taken refuge, then slips away into unconsciousness.

It is still night. The same night? Or a succession of nights later? She does not know. But intermittently, like still shots captured by a camera, the light before sunrise flashes weakly on dim shapes in the surrounding dark. Something white. Rigid with water. Hanging in space. Something solid and shadowy. Sloping up. To a prison-like wall. Low, deformed outlines. Other abandoned cars. A huddle of dustbins. Empty bottles. Glinting in the light. And windows in a threatening building emerging higher and higher as the night retreats. Should she have left this place?

Somewhere above the ground she sees a movement that brings a further rise of panic. To move back or to stay? It becomes the movement of little feet padding down towards the space in which she hides. Little feet in ballet shoes. The hem of a nightdress? Reaching down to the ankles. Soft grey. Like the pursuing day. Frothing softly around the ankles. A child comes into view, pointing a soft clad foot to the step below.

Had she seen the child last night? Waiting to come down? Was she to come all the way down? Now in the lightening day? All the way down the steps. Close to where she lay, some part of her at peace, some part of her frantic beneath the car.

Imprisoned in the cage formed by the child's fingers she sees a dove. The child's face, piquant and sweet, nestling close to the dove. The dove, quiescent against her breast. All grey like the morning sky. The dove, the dress and the dancing shoes.

The child and the dove touch the ground. The child tiptoes over the puddles with the dove nestling in its prison. Pirouettes on her toes. Releases the dove. The dove floating to the ground. Coming close to where she lay straining not to lose consciousness. The dove watching timidly near her hand. The girl feeling the impulse to touch it. Needing to feel its warmth and softness. Missing the comfort of a human arm about her shoulders. Reaching out and feeling the cold hard stone wall. All around her. The wall. Four paces away from her. On every side.

Nana and Devi

It was the middle of the day and Nana and the girl Leloba were sitting in the shade on the deserted beach, when Devi walked up to the rondavel on the hillside and sat in its shadow watching them.

Devi was now grey haired, but the water at Blue Waters Bay was still that brilliant, inky blue; the sun still scintillated off its surface the way it, and they, had danced about when they were girls, from one end of the beach to where the eye could barely see, on sand that still had that buff coloured, dry look. The sand dunes still surreptitiously changed shape before her eyes, forming restful, pleasing contours. Nothing changed, only she. Everything intact as she left it, but for broken sea shells, even up here on the path around the rondavel. They felt brittle and sharp underfoot. And to ageing eyes trying to avoid them, it was like looking for faded jewels in one's past.

In those days she and Nana were habitual thieves, stealing picnics here at Blue Waters Bay every year when the lawful picnickers were away. Did Nana still traipse down here with the girl when they had the beach to themselves? Did the ice cream vendor and hot dog man still accept the economics of keeping away out of season? Was the guard who chased them away still holidaying in Port Elizabeth? Even so, Nana and the girl were careful not to pitch a tent that might be seen from the road. They carelessly draped blankets over the branches of some bushes, hiding there while the sun was hot, while Devi sat in a rush chair outside the thatched rondavel, having come to take her daughter back with her, praying they would come up before dark.

And they did. Nana did not expect Devi to look for her at Blue

Waters Bay, but she always knew Devi had to be told about her daughter. Coming up the hill from the beach, arms intertwined, jumping playfully to avoid chipped sea shells, Nana and the girl Leloba momentarily glanced up towards the hill and discerned the blur of pale green blossoms on Devi's sari. Nana was immediately on her guard.

When Devi stood up with arms extended to embrace Nana her cheap polyester sari slipped from her shoulder, but Nana saw only the skin, the hair, the eyes, that had the look of a sunflower deprived of sunlight. Touched to the point of tears, Nana nevertheless avoided her friend's embrace.

Devi's face, once serene and calm, now crumpled as she lost control in trying to speak, 'After fifteen years, you're not overjoyed to see me, Nana?' And Nana regretted not having told Devi while she was in prison, that her daughter would never return to her.

Because the girl Leloba was not from their shared past, they each felt constrained with her there. Saying very little, the two childhood friends collaborated in the ritual of drinking tea, passing crude utensils back and forth, asking monosyllabic questions, smiling weakly each time their eyes met, but for the most part, gazing unseeingly into the orange scented liquid.

Nana was soft spoken. She now wore unflattering spectacles because she read late into the night in a house still waiting for electricity but was too busy to complain. She practised as a psychologist in the city.

Wanting to reach Nana, Devi took Leloba's hand in both of hers, saying, 'Has your Mama told you about our picnics at Blue Waters Bay?' when Nana interrupted, 'I don't tell her about things that happened before she was born.'

But Leloba, feeling the tension between the women, said with a brittle laugh, 'Not true, Antie! Mama told me Blue Waters Bay was like home to your crowd! Before they declared it white! We come here every year.'

Devi clutched the girl's hand tightly, gratefully, saying, 'So did we. When we were teenagers. Did your Mama ever tell you about one accident . . . when we were here?'

'Did someone drown, Antie?'

For the first time Devi laughed, throwing her head back with complete abandonment. 'No! How could we drown, when we all swim like little fishes. I mean the accident with the blue bottles. You know Blue Waters Bay is full of blue bottles.'

'Mama told me too, too many stories about blue bottles.'

'Did she tell you the one about a boy stung three times on the same day?'

Again Nana interrupted, 'These days we don't have Indian friends.'

Strangely to the girl who looked sharply at her mother, Devi ignored the remark. She leant forward conspiratorially and said, 'I'm the sister your Mama never had.'

Leloba looked from one to the other. The two women were sitting like strangers, one consistently making loving overtures, the other instinctively rebuffing her, yet the girl, through her confusion, felt strangely happy to see them together.

Leloba said, 'I don't want to be rude, Antie . . . but Mama won't tell me which one of her friends you are.' To which Devi simply said, 'Yes.'

Although the tea had just been drunk, Leloba went outside to fill the kettle with water. She instinctively felt the two would overcome their inhibitions if she left them alone. But even with waiting outside the rondavel, watching the tide come in, to give them more time alone, she heard no words exchanged between them, and found them sitting in meditative silence when she came tentatively back inside.

Devi seemed to prefer having the girl with them, for as soon as she entered the rondavel, Devi turned to Nana and asked, 'Why are you not happy to see me, Nana?'

'Yes, Mama. Kiss Antie, please!'

At this Nana faltered, 'I . . . It's such a shock . . . I'm . . . I'm not prepared' . . . and she sat back, withdrawing into herself, as if she had postponed something she dreaded.

It grew dark quickly in the rondavel because the thatched roof was low and the square holes for windows were near the thatch. They lit a paraffin lamp with a glass funnel, then they pulled their chairs close to the rough table making the light from the flame play on their beautiful faces, their dark eyes becoming lustrous in the glow. Leloba's face, unlined, expectant and gleaming with copper tones; Devi's, too quick to show pain; Nana's, impassive, revealing nothing of what she felt; each face was touched by the dancing flame.

Seated like this, it was the most natural thing to take out a pack of cards. Leloba shuffled, Devi cut and Nana dealt the cards for *klaverjass* without partners. At odd moments in the game Devi would look appealingly at Nana, Leloba would question them with a glance, and Nana would withdraw further into herself.

It was midnight before Leloba touched each one and said they should sleep.

The two women slept on the floor of the rondavel with the paraffin lamp burning low, Devi using Leloba's sleeping bag, Leloba slinging a hammock from the ceiling. Well into the night the weak flame spluttered, and then only the wick glowed brightly before it, too, was extinguished.

Nana and the girl Leloba were sound asleep when Devi screamed in the dark, waking them. In a panic, with Devi sobbing in the dark, they fumbled for the matches, refilled the bowl with paraffin, and relit the lamp.

'I can't sleep in the dark anymore,' Devi apologised.

For the first time since she had glimpsed the cheap polyester sari from the beach, Nana softened. 'Do you want me to sit up with you?' she asked.

There was no need for Devi to reply. And the question need not have been asked. Their friendship went back that far. Devi closed her eyes. Nana took her hand. The girl Leloba climbed back into the hammock and dropped off to sleep.

Just as Devi was falling into sleep Nana said, in a husky whisper, 'Because I loved him. Because I loved him, fifteen years isn't enough. He was my lover, Devi.'

This was the hurt Devi was not prepared for. It was so unexpected she could feel nothing. Not anger. Not pain. She lay motionless on the floor, her hand in Nana's. Then Devi whispered, 'So my friend . . . we who are like blood sisters . . . my man is her man.'

Nana said, 'You didn't love him. Your marriage was arranged.'

Devi turned her face away. Still she left her hand in Nana's.

'Why tell me now, Nana? Why not tell me fifteen years ago? I've been punished for what I did. Why punish me again?'

'If you loved him – to tell you would only hurt you. I didn't wish to hurt you, Devi. You hurt me, when you killed him . . .

and there was no way I could hurt you.'

'And now?'

'Now you imagine we are still friends. You come out of prison wanting my friendship. Now I can hurt you. I can withdraw my friendship – the way you took my lover from me. The way you hurt me.'

The two women were both upset by the exchange. Nana buried her face in her hands and cried, while Devi sat up on the floor rocking her body to and fro. Then Devi, without turning round, asked, 'Was it you who betrayed me, Nana?' Nana whispered something that was not audible. Devi said again, 'Was it you who betrayed me?'

Nana raised her face. 'Yes.'

This angered Devi. Her face was no longer pained and sorrowing but convulsed with anger. She turned to face Nana, but Nana did not look at her, her face was buried in her lap.

Devi demanded urgently, in an undertone, 'Why, Nana? Why did you betray me? Wasn't it betrayal when you took my husband for your lover? Why betray me twice? Why betray me to the police?'

Leloba stirred, hearing Nana sobbing, and came over to put her arms around her.

Nana sobbed, 'It's this woman. Make her go away.'

Leloba said, 'Antie, I don't understand what's going on . . . but you can't stay . . . you're upsetting Mama. I've never seen Mama like this.'

They drew apart, Devi went to a far corner of the rondavel to wait for morning. When Nana had settled Leloba returned to the hammock.

It was beginning to grow light when Devi stood up and began to wrap herself in her sari. She was weeping throughout. She used the loose fold of her sari hanging over her shoulder to wipe away her tears.

Nana and the girl Leloba both did not want her to go while she was upset, but they were unable to bring themselves to say anything.

Then Devi moved to the chair where she had been sitting that night and in stooping to pick up a brown paper carrier bag her sari slipped from her shoulder. She placed the carrier bag on the uneven table and removed a crocheted table cloth which she presented formally to Nana.

'I made it in that place,' Devi said, 'I came to take my child and to show gratitude to you for looking after her.'

'You know once they separated all of us, I couldn't keep your child in the township. The Group Areas harassed me. Your family . . .'

'I know. My family wouldn't have my child. They were afraid she would grow up . . . like me.'

'An Indian couple took her. When they found out about you, and when your family disowned the child . . . What am I trying to say? Your child is adopted, Devi. And taken overseas.'

Devi reached out for the table. Her hand touched the top and rested there. Her fingers grasped the edge and curled up tightly. She held on for what seemed too long a time, then she collapsed into a crumpled heap of pale green flowers blurring into each other on the floor. Leloba screamed, 'Ma-ma,' while Nana sobbed uncontrollably.

Emerging from her confusion, the girl was unsure which of the two women she should go to. As Devi had not stirred, she bent down to feel Devi's pulse, when Nana said, 'Don't touch her! Don't touch her! She shouldn't have come here pretending she's my friend. I'll put her out when she comes round.'

The girl whispered just one word in chastisement, 'Mama!'

On coming round Devi saw green and blue colours reflecting off a broken bottle as the sun touched it. Nana had moved her out of the rondavel. Devi moved her head and found Leloba and Nana sitting on either side of her.

Leloba put out her hand to touch Devi's forehead. 'How are you, Antie?'

Devi put her hand over Leloba's. 'I can't stop the nightmares.'

Nana said, 'If you kill someone, you're destined to live with a nightmare.'

'Is that why you went to prison, Antie?'

'They said he was an informer. Many more lives were at risk.'

Nana interrupted, 'Don't listen to her. She's mentally ill.'

Devi said, 'If to have a nightmare when you're awake means you're mentally ill, then yes, I'm mentally ill.'

Then Leloba asked Devi to tell her what it was like to be in prison.

'Prison is bad,' Devi said, 'If they let the sunlight in, it might be bearable. But the windows are too high. Everywhere there's electric lights. All electric lights. No shades. I think our minds need darkness. In prison your mind yearns for darkness. Because you can't dream in the light. And if you close your eyes the electric light comes in. Only an evil mind could have dreamt up the idea of prison. No-one loves you in prison – it's like a loveless marriage. It's made by the law. The law keeps you in it. Only the law can free you from it.'

'Then if you have a child from a loveless marriage, you can't love the child,' Nana said.

'So you thought because I killed him, I couldn't love his child?' Devi asked.

Having listened to the two women, Leloba asked, 'How did my father die, Mama?'

Nana answered, 'He died a natural death, baby.'

Leloba said, 'At school they say my father was killed by a woman. Did you kill my father, Antie?'

Devi said, 'I never knew your father.' Then she sat up and rocked herself to and fro.

Leloba said, 'Was my father a police informer, Mama?'

Nana said, 'Your father loved you, baby.'

'Was he a police informer, Antie?'

'Your father was a good man.'

The girl Leloba stood up and wandered down to the beach, troubled.

When they were alone Devi asked, 'Is Leloba his child?'

Nana sighed. 'I would not have a child from him if he wouldn't marry me.'

'Marry you? And divorce me?'

'No, Devi. I wanted him to marry me, before your marriage was arranged. He was a terrible coward. He was afraid. Afraid of his community. Afraid our cultures were too different. Afraid how we'd be torn when our communities were in conflict.'

'You loved him . . . before he married me?'

'Yes, Devi. It was you who betrayed me. You could not even see we were in love. You accepted the arranged marriage while my heart was breaking. You – of all people – you could have given him the courage to marry me.'

'I knew there was someone – only once we were married.

Before that I was never close to him to know. I was not even interested in him. If I knew it was you, I might not have killed him.'

'Might not? Might not, Devi? Can't you even be sure?'

'I'm only thinking of it now, when I am old and my mind isn't quick . . .'

'You tell me we are like blood sisters. You told me all your secrets. We shared the same bed. Ate from the same plate. Who were closer than you and I? But Devi, could I have married your brother?'

It was dusk when the girl Leloba walked up the hill to the rondavel and found Nana and Devi huddled together with a blanket around their shoulders, and, going up to them, kissed each in turn.

Sunflowers

The Island
Christmas Day, 1989

Dear Seodi,

I write hurriedly from the island before transportation. To God knows where. Forgive me my friend, my letters to you weren't intercepted. I never sent them.

Twenty years on, the island is yet another homeland: fixed, insular, dependent – and remote from the traffic in ideas. Only, we are unambiguous prisoners.

For years I tolerated the isolation – with a kind of egotism – seeing myself – redeemer – martyr – heroine of my people; like Prometheus a freeholder, bound to this rock, my life chipping away while the seagulls freewheel overhead.

In fact I am the fool who filched an idea from the masters to broadcast freely among the oppressed, expecting not even the loser's displeasure. Had I been God, I would anticipate outliving this era. But I am human. And they celebrate the knowledge. I've heard them laughing, like Boors, that we hoped to live out our old age in a free state. In defiance my spirit soars overhead with the gulls screeching angrily at those who have abandoned me here. And at night, each night, it plummets with my lust like any shot bird dashed against the rocks.

The masters taste freedom everywhere, Seodi, despite – perhaps even because of – our oppression. Our home – their fatherland, our people – their chattels, like prisoners magnetised to the granite, powerless to weaken their force. Would you deny this is their island, this their time? Its characteristics are theirs. We? We are still the chain gangs – perhaps forever – forced to work where they will send us.

Forgive my bitterness, friend. It's you who believe in God, remember? The nugget of hope I nursed, today, lies stillborn on the rocks.

It began just eight days ago. A youth put ashore. In his late teens, I reckoned. Thin. Dark. With nothing of the man about his features yet. What's remarkable about that? I asked. I've seen children put ashore.

For the first three days he was left – free – to move without hindrance, his chains still with the blacksmith. From the outset he seemed obsessed with us – we four survivors from the trial. You realise, we four are made to keep our distance from the chain gangs. Each time they file past, to work and back, they never wave, they never nod. They just turn their heads to where we stand, each in her isolated yard like officers at the march past of soldiers.

The new arrival would have none of that. He came up to my yard. Hung around the wall. Peered into my face. Followed me about. Obstructed my path. Making it seem – just – to taunt me for being marooned here. He disturbed me, in an odd way. I couldn't be sure if he were unbalanced, making fun of me, or just serving the masters' purpose. I became more and more tightly coiled like a spring unsure of when my release would come. Yet he didn't single me out for this treatment. He did just the same to each of us.

The days are long. Every now and then, the same thought flashed into my mind, the way a bird dives unerringly into a tree and perches there: that the boy marvelled at being here with us. By the end of the third day – I was lost – I believed he was desperate for a sign from one of us.

It's the solitude. All day and all night. Day in and day out. I churn over in my mind a prized thought, like a grain of sand destined to become a pearl, my mind soft, muscular, like the interior of an oyster forced to harbour the intrusion, adding to it layer by layer to protect itself, yet instinctively shutting it off from thieves until it is whole, distinct from me, with an identity of its own. Then, having lost control over it I must watch it assert its own reality, its independence from me. And should I try to prevent its escape, I am taken along with it.

Like a new-formed pearl the thought stayed lustrous

throughout the day: the boy was desperate for a sign from one of us.

It could've grown from an idea that gratified my vanity over the years: the chain gangs are convinced one of us is their leader. Each new arrival searches each face trying to identify us. 'Of course no-one knows,' we reassured each other. 'No-one can distinguish any one of us from the other,' they said, 'how could they? Men born after we were bound for the island.'

Even so I panicked. A rough, unpolished fear worked like an irritant alongside the lustrous thought: I'd no wish to be identified, to be singled out as the ring-leader, meriting special attention from the masters' tyranny. "We gain strength from being equal," my friends urged. "No sign must betray you to the masters or their chain gangs." But, try as I might, I couldn't expel the thought: the boy needed a sign from me.

By the fourth day he was paired up with another islander. Somehow he persuaded this man to co-operate in tormenting me. Everywhere I turned, there they were. I'd catch the clinking sound they made on the rocks, whirl round and find them standing immobile behind me with an air of timidity, humility, respect. But it was a sham! Oh God! I just knew it was a sham. A pretence. Something cultivated to fool me. How I hated them. I sensed their ridicule, rapists scrutinising, through half-closed eyes, women nursing political aims.

But I reckoned I couldn't survive, harbouring such hatred. Little by little I veered towards sympathy for them and what they might've been given different circumstances. Some were only boys. When it irritated me, such insensitivity, such lack of political awareness, I punished myself for glorifying our politics, for failing to identify with the common man. Like this – hating and fasting – I vacillated throughout the day, attempting to form yet another pearl.

At one stage I observed the boy is handsome. Since he is paired with a man, unwillingly, I worried about him. The island is barren; how could it be otherwise – they are all men here, the chain gangs and the masters; yet it spawns a life of ugliness: the power of one over the other, the rifles over the chains, the physically stronger chained man over the weaker; the latter in pairs, each pair to a blanket, lacking a moment's privacy. We four, on the other hand, existing in awesome solitude, aware we are protected from the masters and the chain gangs, just as long as both groups remained there balancing each other's force.

That night I dreamed I stood over the youth clothed in shimmering colours, shielded by a black, starless sky, my fists clenched in prayer, imitating the blacksmith pounding the boy's body, his head, his face. I woke in a sweat.

And then two days ago – as if in answer to my prayer – Ngoma visited. You know, he always brings me flowers. One from each child. One from him. This time he brought just three – sunflowers. Why sunflowers, I wondered. Why not four?

My mind fluttered about like a soft, blind bird crashing dumbly against the interpretation of this development.

I'd no way of knowing. You recall, we refused the masters' language. They refused us ours. Over the years Ngoma and I have always just stared at each other. The masters stand alongside – listening to our silence. One always receives my flowers. Patiently he plucks each petal, exposing the essential parts. Like a violation of innocence. The action never fails to make me tremble for every woman.

That day Ngoma's face had the patient look of a man anticipating nothing. My first thought was the unlayered irritant: he has taken another woman. Ngoma has always been handsome. You were in love with him first, remember. I? I am for life, out of his life. My love shrivelled, my passion frustrated over the years.

Instinctively the first layer was added: could I blame him? My eyes resting on every aspect of his face, as if touching him in a prelude to love making found no sanctuary there. How could I blame him?

The irritant resumed its work. Look again at the photograph of me in circulation, Seodi. Mine is an unremarkable face, wouldn't you say? But why does no-one remark the unmistakable look of reproach on my face? Because they have forgotten me. My people have forgotten me. Did I expect too much, Seodi?

And so the two lodged alongside each other; one a fully formed pearl, the other still capable of hurting me.

I began this morning as I always have, naming my ancestors, then named the day, the month, the year. A baptism without prayer. When the first fever came I lost count of the days. The masters refused to tell me. The second fever they administered something – one cycle followed immediately after the first.

Had you been here today you would've pardoned the way the chain gangs behaved when we went for exercise. The stretch is monotonous. They seize upon anything that arrests the boredom – the youth certainly provided that. He was exhilarated – the way we all were at the beginning – but his exhilaration went beyond that, as if he were high on some drug. He had that wild elated look in his eyes, of the daggha smoker. I puzzled over what they'd given him. Everyone else stared while he performed all kinds of antics to draw our attention. At first I looked away. It irritated me to see one of us like this. Then I cursed – his mother, his father, his ancestors. It was glorious to hear my own voice resounding in this joyless place. I hoped then he would stop pestering me.

He persisted. He followed me in his usual way, stopping when I stopped, looking timid when I confronted him, while the chain gang, too far away to speak to us, stopped every now and then to shout a loud remark or just to shake their heads and laugh, indulgently, as if we were two lovers who had quarrelled – throughout that morning.

I began the stoning. My companions scolded, in low voices they muttered their disappointment, but failing to restrain me, they kept our agreement. Without enthusiasm and grumbling loudly, they picked up stones and tossed them half-heartedly in the boy's direction. They wouldn't let me be singled out for punishment. The boy didn't miss this. His face registered surprise, then recognition, then unmistakable joy.

I could still have called a halt, Seodi. But my mind shut tight, rejecting another intrusion. I was drunk with egotism. Suddenly I wanted everyone to acknowledge my leadership. Letting go of the stone I raised my fist in the salute and chanted our freedom slogans.

I was blind to their reaction. Their voices clamoured for me to stop, but to my ears it sounded like an ovation, the salute gives me so much inner strength. The boy had wanted this.

He'd thrown himself down, shielding his head throughout the stoning. Now he stood up, watching me, the leader singled out from the rest. The masters came running up to us, gathering in a circle around us on the rocks, their rifles ready.

Then I realised we were all of us standing with fists raised giving the salute. Even the chain gangs whom I despised for their lack of political awareness. We were united, protecting each other. When the masters fired into the air – only then the obstinate wave that took me in its stride subsided. I feared for my people.

Only the boy hadn't raised his fist. For some reason he hadn't responded to my leadership. To the masters it appeared we were saluting him. Each in his turn, with precise, barbaric movements, rifle-butted the boy repeatedly to the ground while your most merciful God stood by – 'with ah! bright wings'.

This afternoon on the march to the quarry someone up ahead scrawled a word in the sand. Some pre-arranged disturbance caused the file to halt so we four could pass and glimpse the word. Today the word was – 'Nyana'. I stumbled. No-one moved to help me. The chain gangs limped past. Each man looked protractedly in my direction, then deliberately dropped a pebble into the lines on the sand, accentuating the word – Nyana. The tail enders weren't erasing the word. The masters would see. I felt then so like a bird flapping wildly around a room as I tried to escape the meaning of Ngoma's three sunflowers.

The son Ngoma and I kept hidden with you these twenty years – Nyana – died this morning on the rocks. Only you know how he came to be here on this island, Seodi. You remember how Ngoma took the new born baby, lifted him high and proclaimed – 'Nyana – this is my son,' before entrusting him to you? Break it gently to him.

Now my mind without a single thought has become like a sunflower on a stretch of desert sand straining for the sun, the sky covered over with brass and iron.

Amandla

PS: Was it Christmas, today?

Two Women

We were sitting forlornly on the dusty shoulder of the Great North Road somewhere in Africa, handcuffed to each other. A little distance away, standing squat in the middle of the strip-tarred road, a car exuded spiralling coils of smoke. All around the day was bright, hot and still. We were stranded.

Luckily for us it was hot and dry: the roads being utterly simple, wide expanses of pink sand without road markings, warning signs, or mileage posts. The same sand which billowed about anything that moved during this dry season became pliable mud, changing shape with the direction of the running water when it rained.

In the wet season, driving became a test of one's ability to avoid potholes, to drive with one wheel on the strip tar while a car approached from the other direction, and to steer into a skid. Naturally, only dare devil motorists used the roads during the wet season. Since there was a stockpile of dare devil drivers, our chances of finding help from a passing motorist in the dry season were negligible.

Unhappily for us it was the period of one of the countless emergencies that marked our country's history. Loyalties to state and race were encouraged to come to the fore, numbing our sensitivity to each other's character.

The woman I was handcuffed to was my captor. When she chanced upon me snapping the barbed wire fence separating her farm from a neighbouring country, I was on the lookout for soldiers, patrol guards, policemen with dogs – everything but a white woman routinely checking the boundaries of her farm.

I was naïve, simple, immature. Idealism duped me into believing a woman would never point a rifle at another. Worse still, I believed in soul force: to escape I should not use passive methods but neither could I use force against another person.

Her rifle was standard protection for a woman living on an isolated farm – a defence against intruders – men, never women. My laugh was nervous and unhappy. 'I'm a woman,' I said, stating what was not obvious. My hair was cropped short and I was wearing baggy trousers and jumper, without so much as a curve to conceal; my own mother could have made a mistake.

'There are no women freedom fighters – in the world?' she asked, unnerving me with the notion I was a freedom fighter. My situation became slightly more precarious.

Her accent was not hard to place – English speaking South African. Not the Cape, something of a drawl in the way she spoke. I plumped for Natal. Natal gave me hope. They wished to secede from South Africa, once. 'Ho-nestly! I'm only trying to leave the country without a passport. Doesn't everyone . . . these days?' I held out my hand to greet her.

She stepped back, ignoring my outstretched hand. 'What d'you have – in that?' she asked.

Turning nervously to my holdall that looked like an ugly secret exposed on the ground, I was embarrassed to say. You do not go about telling every white South African pointing a rifle at you that you are carrying an unpublished manuscript when you're leaving the country illegally. 'Sanitary towels,' I promptly replied, enunciating the words the way one would silently mouth a warning to someone on the other side of a room filled with informers, adding, 'Soiled,' as an afterthought.

'Tip it out . . . Go on,' she ordered when I looked astonished. But I was having none of this. '*You* tip it out,' I said. 'I've seen what soiled sanitary towels look like.'

She edged over to the holdall, the rifle still directed towards me. For a second I thought she did have an unfulfilled wish to see someone else's soiled sanitary towels. But then, grinning glee-fully, she stepped roughly all over my holdall with her dung-covered gum boots.

'Charming,' I said. 'Shall we bottle it?'

'Pick it up. Shut-up. And move.'

I stooped, wishing I had not skipped over large passages of *Satyagraha in South Africa*, groped for the bag and yanked it over my shoulder. The smell of dung made me want to throw up.

How does one convince the enemy that one is harmless? She was behaving as if she had been indoctrinated with stories about how violent and dangerous we are. I thought of a way to reach out to her. In my naïve way I was still provocative. 'I've read *The Story of an African Farm*,' I said tentatively, '*Out of Africa* – even *Animal Farm*,' I muttered hopefully.

'Oh ya? And what do Marxists find in such books?'

I lowered my arms. 'You're wrong, sister. I'm no Marxist.'

'Don't sister me!' She prodded me from behind.

To put her mind at ease I began reciting the Lord's Prayer, notwithstanding which the march from the boundary to the farmhouse continued, even with me offering to repeat the prayer in Latin.

I thought about Nelson Mandela accepting imprisonment for himself, refusing to accept release while others are oppressed, and by so doing gathering the force of the whole world about him. That was soul force. But I could not relate that to this situation. Each time I looked round, the woman lurched forward, the rifle hurt the small of my back, and I had to move on.

She was intent on nothing short of handing me over to the authorities. With this in mind she forced me into the motor car, handcuffed our arms together, then drove for miles along a bumpy dirt road until smoke came curling blissfully up from under the bonnet, leaving the two of us, handcuffed to each other, in the middle of nowhere.

'I need a drink,' I said hoarsely.

Smoking imperturbably beside me, she said nothing, but persisted in using her handcuffed arm to smoke, carelessly dragging my thin black arm up and letting it drop down as she puffed on her cigarette. She was fair skinned, robust, and her expression was grim. Dressed in khaki uniform she contrasted strongly with matt black skin in green trousers and jumper.

Softly, I began to curse myself. 'Fool! Nut case! Simpleton!'

'Who meid?' she asked drily, 'You or me?'

'You'll wash *my* clothes before *I* become your meid!' I retorted.

I was afraid I would doze off, with the smoke from the cigarette hanging listlessly in the air between us, the heat from the sun and the dryness in the air.

'Someone will come along, meid! Don't worry. We'll have you locked up before sunset.'

The only people with cars around here would be soldiers and farmers, all without question friendly to this woman and not to me. I could easily disappear into the bush and be helped by the villagers, if this woman was not sharing a handcuff with me. I knew I would have to resort to force to escape, yet I doubted that I was capable of that.

'You have the rifle. You have the handcuffs. You have the keys. *Do* something, woman! There are villages down there.' I made a sweeping movement with my free arm.

'Who will help me, I suppose?'

'*I* wouldn't sit here serving myself up for a hungry lion!' I said.

She promptly stood up so that I lurched forward into the dust. With her striding ahead and pulling our handcuffed arms and me stumbling behind, we approached the car.

She used newspapers and an old towel to lift the bonnet and prop it on its support. I stood by letting out deep disinterested breaths, watching my arm being yanked this way and that. Water still bubbled out of the radiator, bringing with it rust that coated the engine as the water evaporated from its hot surface. She went to the boot. I stumbled after her. She brought out a container of water and went back to the engine with me in tow.

It was only then, intending to refill the radiator with water, and reaching out to remove the radiator cap, only then she noticed the radiator cap missing. An expression of pure disbelief crossed her face, followed immediately by one of apprehension as she glanced furtively up into my face.

I did not flinch. I wore the expression of the black woman stereotyped in film and fiction: I stood looking as if I could not tell the thermostat housing from the bleed screws. And this was where the idea on which separate education is based brought about her downfall. She could not, she just simply could not encompass that I could know about the engine of a car. She dismissed the idea from her mind like you can drain the cooling system of every drop of coolant. And I felt pity for her.

Before setting out with me, her catch, she had stopped to check the water, oil and battery level in that order. Mundane things that even unmechanical men who drive cars have to do.

At one stage, I casually rested my free arm on the cool radiator pretending total absorption in what she was doing. Then, when she reached up to dislodge the metal support and close the bonnet, I removed my arm, taking with it the water cap, which I let drop casually from my hand as my arm lay along the open window frame of the car that was transporting me to the authorities, just a few miles before the car began to smoke. I saw it roll into the bush.

I could have removed the oil cover but we might have reached our destination before it had the effect I wanted. It had occurred to me to disconnect the spark plugs – she would have been at a loss to reassemble them because they were unnumbered – but that would have left me at the farmhouse where she could have telephoned for help.

Now with a worried, preoccupied look, she motioned with the rifle to the road ahead. We began walking.

A drop from the shoulder of the road would take me into the bush. It stretched on either side of the road, densely packed, dark green bushes.

'A fair-minded woman would let me go,' I said. 'You need only wait in the car for help.'

'While you round up some nasty guerillas, hey meid?'

She had not learnt her history. 'Louis Botha was a guerilla! So was Smuts! Meisie!' I muttered.

I guessed she was looking for a fork in the road, hoping for an added chance of some passing pedestrian, cyclist or motorist who would take a message to someone in the distance. She had not telephoned anyone since capturing me so we were not expected to arrive anywhere until we actually turned up. My freedom depended upon unlocking the handcuffs. Should my freedom hinge on her assistance? Should I not free myself without having to convince her I was not a freedom fighter?

'This is like picnicking in a wild game park,' I said. 'Insane!'

'Then you have the African version of the mad hatter's tea party!' she said.

'Quiet like this in the bush . . .'

She interrupted. 'Animals need to rest too.'

'They're sitting pop-eyed in the bush waiting for something to pounce!'

'I know this part of the country. I was born on that farm. So was my mother and her mother.'

'Would you like me to travel to Europe and say what you've just said?'

'I've no connection with Europe.'

'Europe feels its connection with you.'

'Your sort will drive us into the sea.'

'Unnecessary. Any group of animals isolated from the mainland becomes extinct.'

We walked together for almost an hour. All we found was a monstrously large pancake on the road. 'Elephant dung!' I shrilled, unable to contain a hideously gleeful note in my voice.

'Merely crossing the road,' she said, her voice sounding calm.

Nevertheless, she abruptly turned without further comment and we retraced our steps. An elephant in the vicinity would return at sundown to some watering hole nearby.

We had hardly taken a dozen steps before we were quickly and soundlessly overtaken by a man without shoes who seemed to have appeared from nowhere. We shouted and called to him, half running to catch him, offering him cigarettes, beer and money. Without any indication that he had seen or heard us he maintained his pace with the two of us trying to move quickly in unison, our arms getting in the way. We could not keep up with him. He disappeared into the distance while we slowed down dejectedly.

'He'd have stopped if we weren't handcuffed. And if you weren't carrying that monstrous rifle!' I shouted.

'I could've made him stop. Just firing into the air.'

'Why didn't you, smart ass?'

'He'd be naturally sympathetic to you. I can't handle two of you on my own.'

'He's rounding up his friends now. You might as well let me go.'

'Shut up, meid!'

I was delighted to find the man standing like a sentry alongside the car. He carried in his hand a long staff.

I assessed the situation immediately, convinced I had the advantage. The other woman would have the advantage if a soldier, a policeman or a farmer came along. I lost no time trying to discover which language he spoke. Rapidly I began speaking to him in the dialect commonly understood in that region. He smiled and shook his head at me. I tried again. No success. Now I was beginning to feel disconcerted.

Then, the cheek of the woman, she murmured a phrase in one dialect. He shrugged. She whispered another phrase. He seemed apologetic. Yet another phrase. He concentrated. She did not give up. She tried again. He shook his head helplessly. Then she said something and he beamed at her. She took out a packet of cigarettes. He crossed his legs and lowered himself on to the dusty road. I was appalled.

I had done it often enough, but now I experienced the discomfiture of being in the company of people persistently speaking a language I did not understand. These two sat chatting together for more than an hour, totally oblivious of me. From the expression on the man's face each time he looked at me I could tell they were talking about me. For he kept looking at me. Shaking his head with disapproval. I could just imagine what the woman was telling him. That I was a terrorist perhaps, a criminal, a murderess? For his eyes occasionally opened wide in astonishment as if they could not accommodate the horrific picture I presented to him. And then on something the woman said, he would throw his head back and roar with laughter.

I interrupted them with explanations – in the dialect I knew was used in that area – of who I was. Why I was trying to leave the country without a passport. Of how kind I was. I asked the man to look at my face, see the gentleness there. Why, I could not bring myself to strike this big strong woman with any of the huge stones lying around the roadside. But to no avail.

So I threw handfuls of sand at them, into their hair, into their eyes, down their shirts, just to disrupt the flow of their conversation, to stop them becoming too friendly.

When he finally stood up I could not help feeling relieved to see him go. Though with him went my one chance of escape without force. He dropped down from the edge of the road into the bush and was gone. I wondered if she had sent him with a message to the immigration post.

Escape again depended on overpowering this woman by striking her and searching for the key to the handcuffs.

A group of birds fluttered in unison out of the bushes. We turned around anxiously to see the man reappearing with a bowl and a water bag – the kind of coarse canvas bag people hang outside cars that somehow manages not to drip and still keeps the water ice cold. Still thinking there must be a common bond between us, I looked up at him part expectantly, part gratefully, as he poured a cool stream of crystal clear water into the wooden bowl. I had not reckoned on what his impression of me must have been. With a look in my direction half quizzical, half speculative, and a quick cross shake of his head, he muttered something to the woman and they laughed together.

He handed the bowl to her, she accepted and drank deeply from it. My first thought was that apartheid had succeeded. Glancing in my direction, both of them still smiling, she asked him a question with her eyes. His smile deepened. He retrieved the bowl and offered it to me. I looked up into his face. He pushed the bowl nearer to me. With a quick furious movement I struck at it sending it out of the man's hands and rolling down the road. 'Naughty! Naughty!' he scolded, in English, running after the bowl, brushing off the dust, waving, then dropping once again off the shoulder of the road into the bush.

It was impossible to fathom what this woman's intentions were. She seemed willing to sit like a hitch hiker waiting on the road. She must know the time the guards at the border post changed. I could not say whether she would use the rifle. She had not used it before. There were a number of large boulders lying alongside the road. I might succeed in stunning her, but I would have to be very angry to be capable of this act. Yet the fear remaining with me was that were I to be taken into custody no-one would hear anything further about me back home.

It was while I was actively checking the possibilities in this way that we heard in the distance a humming sound. It would be several minutes before we saw the dust cloud. In this desperate situation both of us panicked.

'If they're soldiers approaching, I'll be imprisoned. I've done nothing wrong,' I said.

Very calmly she then handed me the keys to the handcuffs, saying, 'Here.'

I was young and cocksure about every damn thing. Separate education had a stranglehold on me too. I had never imagined she would offer me the keys. But immediately I assessed her – wrongly. She was so confident the vehicle would bring friends, police, soldiers. She was being magnanimous; from the pinnacle of superiority. So without any hesitation I quickly extended my hand. She closed her hand over the key.

'Give me the radiator cap. That's fair exchange,' she said.

I showed I was puzzled.

She said, 'That's not a military vehicle coming. There isn't one expected until tonight. 7.35 p.m. I must get away. Whichever way – one of us will be raped.'

A feeling of nausea came over me. I buried my face in my hands and mumbled, 'I . . . I . . . I threw it away! Miles back. On the road!'

'You bloody fool!'

I was a fool. Why had I refused to bargain my way out of the situation? Because I had not considered that she could be in danger on this road – I felt I had nothing to bargain with. If she were caught with me now, I would be a party to whatever was done to her. As the horror of the situation hit me, I saw the woman slump over on to the ground and lie motionless. The man had put something into her drink.

The dust cloud could be seen. I first unlocked the handcuffs, before rolling the woman over the edge of the road. Then, jumping into the car, I released the handbrake and pushed it into the bush, then jumped off the shoulder myself.

Innocents

I

We were drinking sundowners; sitting apart from the other hotel guests in a kind of beer garden shaded by trees; morosely smoking; hanging back from speaking; acting as if we had taken a vow of silence: Marya, Beauty and I.

We three were strangers, pretending this holiday friendship was the most natural thing for us. It was not. It would fizzle out the moment we recrossed the border.

The night before we had quarrelled. Each quarrel precipitating another, until last night when we were left devastated. To help clear the air we agreed to climb the mountain.

We set off at sunrise that morning, with several other guests in tow. Shunning the trappings of the male explorer, we wore denim jeans, out-of-shape sweaters, trainers and traditional cone-shaped basket hats with decorative loops on the peak. The mountain was Thaba Bosigo.

To visitors like us it was simply the place where Moshoeshoe, in flight from the turbulence of Shaka's reign, fought off the British, then settled with his people.

We climbed in a leisurely way, not attempting to set a record or to prove this or that, or to be the first to the top. Every now and then we rested, took photographs, picked samples of flowers and leaves, and looked under rocks for unclassified insect life: it was still possible to discover forms of life that had not been identified.

We straggled to the top at two minutes to twelve – I checked my watch. Beauty led us down a path that led to a grey haired man cooking a chicken over a fire. He looked round without surprise. How could he have been expecting us? Yet he rushed forward to greet us as if we were late. He made a gesture with his hand over his abdomen, and I imagined he thought we were hungry. But he turned to a large cauldron standing in the shade and scooped out tins of freshly made beer which he handed round.

There were few tins. So we had to share, our lips drinking from the same tins, touching the same rims, the elderly white guests, and Marya, with Beauty and me. We stood around drinking. Looking about at the group I wondered, were these people testifying that they were law-abiding citizens? That it was only the law which stopped this socialising across the border? This meeting of lips? This drinking of wine from the same cup? Why else should they do it so naturally here and not in South Africa? Were they not responsible for making the law there?

Beauty then led us to a place a little distance away where we could rest in the shade. It was as we were settling ourselves down on the patchy grass growing beneath a tree that we saw the women approaching along another path. It was like entering a theatre at the moment the performers were coming on to the stage.

They were strangely silent. Perhaps the beer made the silence seem remarkable at the time because we were light-headed. The mountain air cleared the bad atmosphere between us. The women settled on the ground with us. Later I remembered that the old man had not greeted them.

One woman sat apart from us, her face turned away. Being the youngest, Beauty went to her in the customary way with an offering of drink. But the woman covered her face with her scarf. Her companions called to Beauty, who returned, abashed, and sat down. I mistakenly thought it was because Beauty was with Marya and me that the woman rebuffed her.

Then Beauty said, 'Wethu, may I tell these others?' and the woman called Wethu said, 'You tell and I'll put you right.'

Beauty brought two rush seats for herself and Wethu and began speaking to us.

'She went home to her mother,' she said, indicating the solitary woman, 'to give birth to her first child. As is the custom.'

'But also because if the child were born where her man was

working the child would not have been registered a citizen of their home country,' Wethu said, leaning forward on her stool.

'Yes, the law is applied differently to people of different races. Her sister married a man of the other race and gave birth to her child just in the place where they found employment. And their child was made a citizen of the home country,' Beauty went on.

'But they wasted time trying to find out if the law was changed while they were abroad.'

'By the time they discovered it was unchanged, she was in her eighth month of pregnancy.'

'The midwife advised her not to travel.'

'But they were afraid the child would not be a citizen of any country if it were born abroad. So they made arrangements and travelled homeward on foot. That's right, no?' Beauty asked.

'Yes. The journey was distressing to her. The roads were through rough country. It was dangerous to stop by the road. She could not sit about when she needed to. They stopped where they found people and public houses. But the lavatories were barred to them wherever they stopped.'

'Because they were not of the other race,' Beauty repeated.

'In the eighth month she needed to relieve herself frequently. The baby put pressure on her bladder. Walking for long periods of time, she had difficulty when they stopped, in rising from the ground. On the second day her waters broke.'

'They had passed a hotel a few yards back,' Beauty said.

'But they were refused a room,' Wethu said. 'The staff who were of their own race apologised and were sympathetic.'

'They said even they were not allowed a bed when they did the night shift.'

'Nor were they allowed to eat or drink on the premises.'

'When she asked where they were allowed to sleep, the staff were embarrassed and shook their heads.'

'But she said it was time for the baby to be born and they could see her condition.'

'They rushed inside again and appealed to the people who were not of their race to make an exception for the woman about to give birth.'

'They said they would disinfect the room and burn the bedding after she left.'

'Still they refused.'

'The staff were disheartened and reported back to the couple,' Wethu said.

'She said again, "where do you eat and sleep?" '

'After much discussion and much refusal, they took her to a room a little distance away from the hotel.'

'It was of cement, cold in the evening, hot in the day, with cavities for windows and door.'

'It was shaped like a rondavel only made of cement. They didn't mind that. They didn't mind the hens running about, and the birds in the ceiling. It was the bird droppings on the floor – and other things,' Wethu said.

'She asked if she could use the place to give birth and they were humbled by her request. They swept the floor and scrubbed it. They brought blankets, coir matting, and a primus stove to heat the water,' Beauty said.

'Through the night they carried paraffin tins of water which the man kept warm on the stove.'

'The news spread to all the hotel staff – the waiters, the cleaners, the chef and the cooks, the chambermaids, the bar staff – who were all of their race.'

'The men offered candles to light up the place.'

'The women stood around offering encouragement to her. One wiped her forehead. Another held her hand. One massaged her back each time the pain came,' Beauty said.

'She watched the baby coming,' Wethu said.

'The cord was around its neck.'

'They loosened it.'

'And then they saw it was a boy.'

'The news was taken quickly to the hotel, as if they were all family, while they cut the cord with a blade of grass. Their new friends brought the child gifts of used clothes and food which they stole from the hotel for them.'

'They made the final lap home and the family greeted them with an ngoma to mark the baby's birth. They all thought very highly of the man because he married her when the child was not his but the child of her sister's husband,' Beauty said.

'His wife bore him no children. So he wished to adopt the child,' Wethu said.

'But she refused.'

'Because the man had married her knowing the child was not his.'

'She respected him for his attitude to the child.'

'But then it was rumoured the chief heard a child was born to her that was the brother-in-law's child, and that the child would inherit the livestock.'

'The chief was pleased that her brother-in-law had no children because it was the custom in such cases for the livestock to pass to the chief when the brother-in-law died.'

'The chief had already contracted business on the basis of collecting the brother-in-law's livestock.'

'The livestock was considerable because the family could trace their line back to the time when the chief's family began to rule the village. Besides cattle, the stock included horses, fowl, goats, geese and buck.'

'The chief then had it rumoured that a disease was spreading amongst all new-born boys and that the villagers were at risk from the disease.'

'He ordered all new-born boys who had not yet reached their first birthday to be killed.'

'The news of the order was secretly brought to the brother-in-law by someone who knew the chief.'

'The brother-in-law came to visit the couple at night and warned them to take the child away.'

'He was like a messenger from God to them.'

'They left their belongings and fled back to where the husband had been employed before the child's birth.'

Beauty continued, 'The boy grew there until he was of an age when he decided to leave home.'

'His race was still heavily persecuted,' Wethu interrupted, 'yet he travelled up and down the area, crossing into his own country, and back again, speaking with people, giving them reasons to hope.'

'Then he came to the place where his family lived and reported to them that his mother and father were well,' Beauty said.

'They prepared an ngoma for him with delicacies, dancing girls, musicians, and wine made from the juice of sugar cane, inviting all the neighbours.

'Late into the evening while they were reminiscing about

their history someone remembered that he was born in the year of the slaughter of new-born sons.'

'At first they marvelled that he had escaped. They rejoiced that the line would continue. Then they speculated about how he escaped and he truthfully recounted the story of how his parents had been warned. "But who could possibly have warned them?" they asked. "A friend," he replied, "because that is what he was told, his parents not wishing him to know the story of his parentage." "Whose friend?" they demanded to know. "A friend from God," he said. 'You mean a friend of the enemy who killed our sons," they said in anger. "The friend was no friend of ours. Or why did your parents not stop to warn us so we too could make our babies escape?" To this he had no answer. He said it was God's will that he be spared,' Beauty ended softly.

'Even though they were of his own kin, they were suspicious of him since he had survived the slaughter. The neighbours were resentful that he had escaped.'

'One of these reported to the chief that there was a survivor from the slaughter.'

'The chief by now was old, and a little more kindly. His advisers urged him to spare the man since he had survived.'

'These others filled the chief's mind with news of his ideas, that the chief was not the most important chief and that there was hope for them in another country.'

'Pressured by them the chief had the man brought to him. Under questioning he found the man to be reasonable and truthful and would have let him go. But they insisted he had done wrong to the chief in defeating the chief's order. So the chief had him put to death,' Beauty said.

And Wethu added, 'That is why she is sorrowing.'

When the story was told, Beauty appeared at peace with the strangers. They rested in silence around her. Marya appeared stunned. The hotel guests seemed not to comprehend what was expected of them. One by one we fell asleep in the afternoon sun. On wakening, the group of women was gone and the old man lay asleep, where they had been. We asked where they were. Beauty made no reply. We walked around the mountain with Beauty searching for them until dusk, but found no trace of them.

Back at the inn that night we were silent and uneasy. Marya seemed to yearn for the company of the European guests, glancing listlessly in their direction. The incident reminded me uneasily of how little we understood each other.

II

So we resumed sitting in the garden, drinking beer, smoking, thinking separate thoughts, knowing that our time for under-standing each other was about to end: Beauty, Marya and I.

We met at the start of the week. Marya made the first overture. We snubbed her. She kept it up until we held back, then grudgingly allowed her into our circle.

Marya met us openly. This I found to be unbelievable. It seemed only Marya was capable of being open with us. I needed to be open; Beauty must have wanted to be; but only Marya could carry it off.

This seeming accomplishment on Marya's part gnawed at me. How dare she be without suspicion of us? While Beauty and I were uneasy even with each other?

Conscious that the European guests were observing us, Beauty suggested we play at being long lost friends. 'If we act real good, we'll fool ourselves,' she said.

That first day we did have tremendous fun pretending not to be tourists; hiding our cameras in knapsacks toted about on our backs; surreptitiously taking photographs when there were no spectators; stooping to pick and examine flowers when there were any. The whole charade made us break out into fits of laughter that afflicted us at any time of day. That night we called to each other from our neighbouring rooms and laughed until we dropped off to sleep.

But I kept getting the feeling no-one actually knew where it would lead; that if we were honest with ourselves, we would admit feeling uncomfortable thrown together in this way. I did.

Once during that first evening, when Marya stood up to go awkwardly to the bar to order another round of drinks, Beauty, turning to watch her, confessed, 'I'll stay friends, Letschmi – with you and her – only till I can put you on the spot.'

No matter how I pressed her, she would not elaborate, leaving me to comtemplate where this unwanted confidence placed me in relation to Marya and her.

We were together tenuously, Beauty and I, presenting a united front against Marya the Afrikaner, only because of our colour. Alone, we told each other nothing about ourselves except that I was a student, she from the Cape. We revealed nothing more. Beauty was suspicious of me, I of her; and both of us were distrustful of Marya.

It was to be expected: we three were South African.

But the socialising between African, Afrikaner and Indian (which we had never done before) – each wanted to show she could manage it. To Marya we lied, of course. We pretended that we were in agreement on every issue that mattered. She could not know any better.

In spite of this, Marya met us openly.

We were well into the second day before I realised Marya had no reason to suspect us of anything – she knew what we wanted: equality between rich and poor, illiterate and learned, and the vote to bring it about. She had the vote. What she was afraid of was unconditional equality. In actual fact it was she who had to win us over.

Once I realised this my hostility subsided. This led Marya to speak haltingly of her family, as if she had first to purge herself of sin: 'They observe the Sabbath . . . scrupulously. They believe in predestination. But you know these things.'

'How does predestination affect . . . the rest of us?' Beauty asked, not really wishing to know.

Marya hinted subtly at the presence of guilt there somewhere. 'We'll quarrel if I say.'

It prompted me to confess, 'I'm also conscious of my Indian background,' as if to balance the other's inadequacy. 'Hinduism has this caste business.'

Since Beauty was at home in Africa, she took it upon herself to reassure both of us, saying in a flippant way, 'It doesn't show!' as if our race were a blemish, or a dropped hem. 'You could pass for Italian, Letschmi. And you could pass for Norwegian.'

The expression embarrassed us. There was something uniquely South African about it. This Beauty knew. It was why she repeated the phrase. I was beginning to feel hostile towards her.

By the third day we had adapted to the pace and silence of the place: the corrugated ridges that made up the dongas, the green grass burned black to the roots, the brown sand bleached white by the sun; the unexpected scintillating streams of blue water; the sunset colours of purple, lilac, mauve and pink in layers from horizon to zenith; and drinking sundowners in the shade. We were thoroughly like European expatriates in Africa.

I felt uncomfortable. Beauty did not give any sign. But again, Marya succeeded. She made an effort to include us in every activity. She avoided saying anything controversial the way she avoided using the words 'African', 'Coloured', 'Indian'. She went in search of our company with an open-faced, light-hearted, missionary zeal.

But again Beauty scoffed. In one of her confessions she said Marya only befriended us because the other guests were elderly. Then she spoke out; she was at home in Africa. She stated the obvious, 'We'll be pupils learning from you for eternity. Servants. Converts. Someone or other hawking something. Needing your power to sign a form, to grant permission, to give the "okay" to our cause.'

I agreed. I needed no-one to tell me Marya had never socialised with an African or an Indian. How could she have? They taught her to accept a status above ours. But then, neither had I socialised with the other two groups, nor had Beauty. We quarrelled about it.

Funnily, Marya was not put off. Dozing in the sun, she smiled. Inwardly I knew she was gloating. She was secretly convinced – that was the only explanation – that friendship between us was possible without bringing each other's history or politics into it.

Although we remarked upon the satisfaction in her eyes, we did not let on. Beauty and I acted so well we brought hope even to the elderly guests who looked on. Only at times was I unsure. And Beauty remained aloof. Even from me.

By the fourth day, when we began to be relaxed with each other, I noticed Beauty change. She let things pass without being on the defensive. She sat back, detached from the argument, looking pensive, almost despairing, as if the time for discussion had passed. So I rushed in against Marya, unwilling to give an inch.

This led us inevitably to quarrel, and then to climb the mountain.

III

It was the night before we were all to leave, with guests moving around the beer garden exchanging addresses, buying each other a final drink, the three of us sitting morosely, our discussions having destroyed the possibility of friendship, when Beauty broke the silence in a shrill, blasphemous voice, demanding, 'Crisps? Anyone for crisps? Cheese and onion crisps?'

Startled out of our meditation each of us reached out and took a single crisp, then Beauty pranced around the garden offering the bag of crisps to the European guests. I watched through half-closed eyes each hand withdraw a crisp. Was this what they meant by sacrilege, I wondered. These Christians.

The European guests, as if caught up in some robotic activity, followed Beauty's lead.

The bag of crisps was empty. Now Beauty stopped in the centre of the garden demanding – why are we starving in Africa? – as if she were the teacher and they would chant back the answer. The guests rushed to her like a disorderly class offering all sorts of answers about tobacco and coffee and sugar; pastoral farming; unnatural boundaries; and war. Beauty elbowed her way out of the crowd leaving them clustered there babbling to each other. She came to where I sat with Marya and shouted for all to hear, 'Should we work towards one culture, African, Indian and Afrikaner?' – and looking at her I knew Beauty did not want that. The guests swept towards us. But Beauty would not listen. She actually put her hands over her ears. They hung about, feeling unsure. What had disturbed her? Could she be performing?

Beauty was not through. Climbing on a chair she demanded – 'When does African history begin?' This time they thought they knew the answer.

'Before the colonists arrived,' they shouted back with one voice, happy they were in agreement about it.

But she spurned them. She turned away. They could not satisfy her. That was not the answer she wanted. Still they hung around, concerned about her, wishing to establish some rapport with her.

I felt she was looking for a way to broach the topic she wanted to discuss, but could not bring herself to. It was not the question, 'Are women in our world more subordinate than others?' because she still had that distanced look in her face. Nor was it, 'Do we want equal opportunities before we are liberated?' because she was not forthcoming here either. They did not agree an answer to, 'Are marriage laws oppressive?' nor to, 'What is our contribution to world culture?' Yet by now, I could see that these were the things that mattered to her. She distanced herself in a way that left her unapproachable. Each question Beauty threw to us and left the European guests to quarrel over, the way a pack of animals fought over a single hare.

There was no one answer. It was as if Beauty had isolated a hidden motive. We waited for her to exhaust herself. So we sat again in silence in the beer garden.

It was then she mentioned the effect the missionaries had on this part of Africa.

Marya looked about as if to pluck the answer from the landscape. For Lesotho was an arid place for plant and animal life. Yet it overflowed with places of learning – schools, colleges, seminaries, convents – even a university. And everyone spoke fluent English.

But by this time we would not take Beauty's lead. We looked at her sullenly, assessing what she was about, her motives, where she wished to lead us. And Beauty must have seen how she was dominating us yet she would not, or could not, stop. So she said the words I would not say, 'Education is what they brought, the Christian missionaries. Not Christianity.'

I disagreed. The nature of the schooling led inevitably to a seminary for the priesthood or brotherhood for young boys and to a convent for young girls. We spent most of the week visiting the nuns, the brothers, the monks, in these places. They came with Christianity.

And so Marya asked, 'You mean then that Christianity is out of place in Africa?'

'Christianity followed hard on the heels of the explorers – or was it the other way round? Beauty asked self-consciously.

'The Bible and the gun,' I chipped in, ignorantly.

Then Beauty made the statement she had wanted to make all week. 'Christianity belongs in Africa,' she said.

I was bemused, disappointed with this line. After all our

discussions, this was a let-down. I gained courage from her silence. I accused her of being afraid of Marxism. Of being intellectually colonised.

She asked what I knew of the early Christian Church. I knew nothing. She said with passion, 'Africa was an integral part of the early Christian church, before it was moved from Carthage to Rome. All colonies were ruled from Europe,' she said, 'so the Romans moved the church to Rome from Carthage, once Christianity became popular.'

'What difference does that make?'

'By doing that the Church became associated with Europe.'

'If the Church had remained in . . .'

'Carthage.'

'. . . Yes . . . whatever the place is – how would that have changed things?'

'Our input into the early Church would be recognised!'

'Go on.'

'That's it.'

'I'm Hindu. What input?'

'Even Christians don't know what our input was.'

'Tell me, then!'

'Look it up, Letschmi. For my sake. Begin with the early Popes. Then check out St Augustine – the one who wrote *City of God*.'

'Augustine was a Roman!' Marya protested.

'Like you and I and Letschmi are South African. Like Martin Luther King was American!'

'You're a racist!' Marya said.

'No, no. I'm a member of my race when my people don't leave written records, when we lose control of the land. But I'm a member of a nation when you want to hide the fact that my race has achieved something. The Popes in the early Christian Church were from Africa, when the Christians were being persecuted. Victor, Gelasius, Melchiades, they were African Popes. We had a Synod of North African Bishops. St Augustine was an African.'

That was how Beauty got us to where she wanted us to be. Marya and I sulked about that night. There was no sound of laughter on our corridor. At two that morning, unable to sleep, I went to Beauty's room. I found Marya already there. The three of us talked until the daylight hours.

We crossed the border together. Beauty was taken off the train. We left the train and waited for her. But they detained her. When I said goodbye to Beauty, I promised her that if I did not look it up, someone else would.

The Seed

I

The seed should have been planted along with the rest in the arid, rust red soil. Instead it lay gleaming on the toughened skin of the old woman's palm like a hardened black tear drop. She had held it back.

She was stooped in the manner of a large old woman, feet set wide apart, legs awkwardly bent, with an arm along the sloping length of a thigh supporting her weight. All morning she had moved up and down the rows in this half-bent posture forcing each seed into the soil with her thumb, while the sun rested shimmering on the earth. Now, with the sun poised regally in the blue sky overhead, her hand clenched tightly around the one remaining seed as she stretched forward to draw the rust covered implements she had been using towards her. When she straightened up she brought with her a shovel and hoe, brushed her hand on the loose, heavy, blue cotton dress she wore, then stood quite still.

Was it the frustration of planting seeds where none would grow that had made her hold this one back? Slowly the clenched fingers relaxed. The fist unfurled. Cradled in her palm, the black seed glistened with perspiration from her hand. Of the seeds she had planted, some would not swell with water; some would grow stunted; some would look sickly with disease; and all would wither with the first sign of drought. Having held it back, would she want to force this seed's passage through life, uncovered by the soil? With a decisive movement she delved into a pocket of her blue dress and groped for a handkerchief, a corner of which she knotted around the seed with brisk, determined fingers. She carried the shovel and hoe to the end of the field where she had begun sowing and propped the shovel up on its blade in the soil near a metal bucket of water. She returned to the field taking the hoe with her. Then, moving backwards along the rows in a slow, preoccupied way, drawing the hoe towards her as she moved, she covered the newly sown black seeds with the dry red soil.

When she paused during the blistering heat of the midday sun it was to ask herself, was it perhaps the irony of planting seeds at her time of life that had made her hold this one back? For was she not like this homeland, the life ebbing from her? She too could no longer retain life in her. She touched the handkerchief in her pocket. Then again, was she not like the seed, tough and resistant?

She resumed her work, walking up and down the rows; stamping firmly down on the newly covered seeds; sprinkling water in handfuls from the bucket on to the soil; stopping only when there was just sufficient left to cool her face and neck and to rinse the sand off her feet.

At the end of the day when the old woman left the soft surfaced red field with the tools on her shoulder and the empty bucket in one hand, she wore a man's pair of old, inflexible white cricket boots. As she walked she sang to herself in a soft, mellow voice, while the sun receded indifferently into the background.

II

That night, with red and violet streaks in the sky where the sun had been, the old woman drew the child on her lap closer to her, as they sat around a communal fire. But he would not have her sing him to sleep. Her own drowsiness she fought off, in response to his plea, 'Make a story, Armah. Make a story.' A plea which was soon picked up and tossed from one voice to another across and around the crackling fire until the old woman began to weave a story about a seed that failed to grow.

'The seed,' she said, 'was buried with many, many seeds just like it – in rich dark earth – where all seeds grew in the way that was expected of them. But, of all the seeds buried in the earth that season, only this one failed to grow.'

'Say what seed it was, Armah,' the child said, in an encouraging tone, as if she needed to be coaxed to elaborate on any detail.

'To make what difference, Jelani?' a voice spoke querulously from the darkness.

The child turned an uncertain, uncomprehending look towards the speaker while the light from the fire played across his face. The old woman, observing the child, remembered the little girl who had sat like this on her lap years ago asking the same question. Then the old woman had said the seed was just like every seed that grew in the way every seed grew in that part of the province. The girl's need for detail remained unsatisfied. Like the boy she believed they all knew the name of the seed, but, in the manner of adults, withheld it from her. Now the old woman said, 'If I name a woman, that woman could grow powerful, she could grow beautiful, she could grow wicked, she could grow kind. If I name the seed, it can only grow to be one kind of plant.'

The child thought about this, then reached up and kissed her cheek.

'Now, where the seed should have grown, there was a wide gap in the row,' she continued. 'Each time the planter passed the gap, he became a little bit anxious, a little bit cross and a little bit disappointed.'

'Was he worried about the seed, or was it just that the gap was untidy?' the child asked.

'He was tidy man! He swept the field each day!' someone shouted with delight.

The others joined with him in laughing and teasing the boy. They were a group of middle-aged men and women sitting on unmatched chairs and makeshift stools, some smoking tobacco in pipes, some drinking coffee, others drinking home-brewed beer.

When the laughter subsided, someone added, 'Listen, Jelani. If the planter spaced the seeds when they were sprouting he would lose more. Not so, Armah?'

'But he did wonder about the seed,' said another.

'Did he need every seed to grow?' the child persisted.

'Isn't it important that everything grows, Jelani?'

'Not if he was rich!' the child retorted.

'He had enough to eat,' the old woman said quietly.

'Did he own the land, or was he just a worker on someone's land?' he asked.

'Jelani!' someone answered crossly. 'The man was just a planter. Where do you find this boy, Armah?'

'Why did the seed bother him then?'

'Because the planter's life lacked interest,' the old woman said, 'and the seed was different.'

They all waited, expecting the child to want an explanation. Someone stood up to add more charcoal to the glowing fire. When it seemed that he accepted the answer, perhaps without understanding it, the old woman went on, 'So, the planter – he began giving the seed special care.'

'Can *he* have a name?' the child asked.

'*You* say a name for him.'

'Je-la-ni!' he pronounced, without hesitation.

'Yo! Yo!' someone laughed. 'Jelani is a boy! A naughty boy,' he added, 'the planter is an old man.'

'Wait! Wait!' he called. Then, with his eyes closed, he searched for a name while they waited, indulging him.

'Mo-le-ah, then!' he pronounced.

The old woman looked around the faces of those listening, wanting their approval. 'Moleah?' she asked.

They murmured assent.

'On his way home each day – Moleah – gave the seed a little more water. When the days became warmer he shaded the ground from the sun with leaf mould. Moleah waited. Nothing happened. He looked more closely at the earth, and it seemed to him that the spot where the seed would not grow was too sandy. So, Moleah added some manure to help the earth hold on to the water. He gave it more water. Still nothing happened. Some time later Moleah began to fear the water was clogging up the earth just where the seed failed to grow. So, he worked some sand into the soil to help the water flow through. And still – nothing happened.'

'The seed was dead, Armah,' the child prompted.

'No, no. The seed was waiting,' the woman corrected.

'By now, the field was covered with new growth, the leaves just about to turn green. But still, walking carefully between the rows to water the seedlings, the planter – he could not close his eyes to the gap. He fretted and he fussed over this one seed that failed to grow. At night – the planter – he would lie in his hammock wondering will the seed come up through the earth the next day. In the morning he would run out to the field only to find the ground undisturbed.'

'Someone stole the seed, Armah!' the child whispered.

'The planter – he even feared that,' someone said, 'but who steals something with no value, hey Jelani?'

'Knowing the seed had no value – the planter – he nevertheless took his blanket – which was striped red and orange like the sun – and slept alongside the seed – waking with the sun to look upon the earth. Still nothing happened.'

'Only an old man spends so much time with one seed when there are so many,' one woman laughed derisively.

'Even a woman,' the old woman corrected, 'when she values what is unusual.'

'In the end – Moleah – he just had to find out what happened to the seed. So he went down on his knees and with his hands he ·began to dig into the earth – with all his friends standing around laughing and pointing at him. He scooped the earth up, he rubbed it between his palms, he sifted it through his fingers, he repeated this – until he found the seed. Now Moleah – he expected to find a rotting seed because he gave it so much water. But the seed – it was just the way he buried it in the earth – smooth-skinned and shiny. His friends – they stepped back from him a little bit frightened when he held up the seed for all to see.

While they looked in wonder at the seed, a strange idea began to shape in Moleah's mind.'

'The seed was special, Armah?' the child suggested with a sense of wonder.

'The planter – he began to believe the seed was resisting growth.'

A stillness and attentiveness came over the group gathered around the fire.

'Out of respect for the seed's resistance – the planter – he polished the seed until it shone like a semi-precious stone. Then he walked into the town and asked a silversmith to twist an ancient design to hold the seed. The seed in the silver setting was placed in a glass box. The glass box was hung over the fireplace in the planter's cottage.'

They waited in silence in a circle around the glowing embers, until one by one they began to grow restless.

'Poke the fire, Nason. Pour coffee for Armah,' someone whispered, wanting her to continue.

When the old woman spoke it was as if from some distance, 'You sleep now,' she said.

'Armah!' they complained. 'Why does Armah always do this? Please Armah, that's not the end.'

'There are many endings,' she murmured, smiling.

The child's arm crept upwards around her neck. Its softness and warmth reminded her of the hardness of the black seed in her pocket. While he slept on her lap she rested her face on the roughness of his hair and felt an indescribable warmth for the child. Of all the children who had sat like this on her lap, this child – perhaps because of the way he questioned everything – perhaps because he seemed to come alive in the company of older people – it seemed to her this child would expect authority to justify itself. This seed she held back, was it her resistance? Should new life not be planted here? In soil where dormant life is imprisoned within its crust; where the roots are choked; the rising sap stifled; where it seemed appropriate for old women and men to be sent into exile to die?

III

In the field the next day, the old woman laboured without rhythm, halting frequently to stare across the bleak, even landscape. Close to the ground a thick haze, given off by the heat, appeared like a distorting liquid suspended in the air. The air itself felt dry and still. It seemed to her the grains of red sand also hovered over the ground waiting for the first arid breeze to sweep them away exposing the thwarted life buried in the earth. With this image of her surroundings, she went about her work shut in with her thoughts, staring every now and then moment- arily towards the horizon until, at last, she sensed more than saw movement in the distance. With her hands resting on the handle of the shovel she focused on the disturbance until the movement took shape and she recognised the boy running towards her waving a letter.

The letter was simple. 'Armah, how would the child be housed? How could the child be hidden?'

The boy waited near her, panting harshly, while looking up to watch her face. It was only when she had folded the letter and put it back into its envelope that her eyes, resting on him, lost the anxious, concentrated expression that had excluded him. She took his hand and led him away from the field. Near the metal bucket of water she settled down on the ground, before extending both hands to him.

'The seed,' she murmured, as if there had been no break in the story, 'hung by the fireplace in the planter's cottage for many seasons. Then one day, a thief came to the village. He went from one cottage – across the land – to the next – calling through the door to find – was there any work in the fields? He found no-one home. It was the day for a wedding feast in the village. All the planters had walked to the bridegroom's home. Since there was no custom to lock doors – the thief – he wandered unmolested in and out of each cottage. He was free to pick and choose whatever he wished to steal. When he came to the planter's cottage –'

'Moleah.'

'Moleah's cottage – the thief – he couldn't close his eyes to the glass box hanging by the fireplace. You see, Moleah – he had nothing of value. The cottage was completely bare except for the hammock and the glass box. In the quick manner of a thief – he reached for the box – forced open the glass and slipped out of the cottage with the jewel.'

'No, no, Armah! He knew it was a seed,' the boy said, laughing in disbelief.

'How so, Jelani?'

'It *looked* like a seed!'

'Do you put seeds in silver? The thief – he couldn't help it. He believed it was a jewel. You would believe it was a jewel.'

'What name did *he* have?'

'The thief? Seroko.'

'Is something bad going to happen to him?'

'Who has that power to make something evil happen? The thief saw the jewel. He wanted the jewel. He believed it would enrich his life. So he took the jewel. And – everywhere he went – he carried the jewel with him in a soft cotton wallet. Each time Seroko stopped to rest, he unwrapped the cloth, polished the silver and the jewel, then left the jewel to lie in the sun. He travelled from place to place – picking fruit – chopping trees – digging wells – and thieving, travelling into and out of each province – always taking with him the jewel. When he had put together enough money from his work and from thieving, he asked a jeweller to shape a ring for him in the symbol of an ancient God – with the jewel placed in the centre.'

'Why steal and also do work?'

'If he did no work they would know he was a thief!'

'Who?'

'Those who are not thieves.'

'Couldn't he only do work?'

'Work was not as interesting as thieving. Now, people seeing the ring – they whispered amongst themselves – the thief must be the son of a rich chief travelling in disguise through our province. So they treated him like a prince. He was the guest of honour at weddings and festivals everywhere he travelled. Sometimes they asked him to judge a case that needed an outsider if the people were not to become angry with the chief. They allowed him to buy goods just by showing his ring. Soon – through clever trading – he was a rich man.'

'He'll be punished when they find the jewel is only a seed.'

'Who will punish him if everyone is a little bit evil and a little bit good?'

The child said nothing.

'Some years later the thief settled in a community where he was well-respected. One day he hurried to the next town on business but – in his hurry – forgot his ring near the bowl where he washed each day. A few days later, he returned home to find the jewel had begun to sprout. The appearance of the jewel filled him with horror. It seemed to be struggling to grow out of the ancient silver design. He wasn't able to understand what it meant. His first thought was that the ring was bewitched. Although he had never before been without the ring, he now feared if he wore it something terrible would happen to him. When his family and friends asked him, 'Where is the ring?' he said, 'It is stolen,' because he suspected that something evil would happen to them if they looked at it. It seemed to him a sign that he was to lose all his wealth and the people he loved. With all these fears in his mind, he spent a great deal of time running back to his room to look at the jewel. As the days went by he began to worry that the sprouting jewel might need some water. So, very reluctantly, he sprinkled a few drops of water on the seed. Then he placed the ring on the window-ledge where the sun would fall on it. Very slowly he began to consider that the jewel was a seed. Now he feared that if he tried to remove the growing seed from its silver design – that it would be damaged. So – he left the seed in the silver. All the while the seed grew the thief remembered the planter and the glass box. At last – when the leaves were just about to turn green – the thief went to the centre of the busy trading town followed by his friends who now knew about the seed. He dug a hole in the ground and planted the silver ring, with the seed twisted all round it, in the earth. The seed grew slowly into a tree, with silver sprinkled on the underside of its leaves.

'He could take the seed back to the planter,' the child said.

'The seed didn't belong to the planter.'

'He would be glad to know the seed did grow.'

'He might be hurt to know the seed wouldn't grow for him.'

'Was the thief a good thief because the seed grew for him?'

'He was like any thief who steals what someone else values.'

'Did he stop thieving?'

'He thieved in unseen ways.'

'Can you say a name for the tree now, Armah?'

'I don't know a name, Jelani, but I know where a tree grows with silver on its leaves.'

She kissed him. 'Run home quick.'

She remained sitting on the ground watching the child run, then turn to wave, until she lost sight of him. How would the child be housed? How could the child be hidden? What did she mean? Where was she that she could ask these questions? Was she told she could have work if she lived in a room at the back without her child? If she were, then she could ask, 'How would the child be housed? How could the child be hidden?' So what did she mean? That she did not want the child with her? She could not see the value of the child. She could not know he would enrich her life. How could the child go to her if she did not value him? How would the boy understand? How could he understand when he was too young to understand the myth. She could see how he struggled to find the meaning of the myth. But the meaning would never be his while he struggled. It would only be his when he had lived out his life. And he might not have the patience to wait for his life to unfold before the meaning came to him.

IV

'Jelani! Jelani! Jelani!'

The boy had spread on the table before him a meticulously ironed, clean white cotton handkerchief, in the centre of which, conspicuous and isolated, lay Armah's black seed. He looked up from the cloth without a single flicker of anticipation. First he located the voice. Then he identified a woman waving excitedly from the crowd. Only later did he recognise with an effort, and then only vaguely, his mother. He had folded the handkerchief and slipped it away by the time she reached him. Still with excitement and anticipation in her manner, she greeted him with an exuberance that did not falter even when she felt him stiffen unresponsively. That she smelt of flowers, not earth, was his first assessment of her.

He accompanied her solemnly through the city, checking himself from responding with wonder at the mechanical movement around him. He watched a door slide open when he stepped in front of it. He stood in a train where there seemed to be only standing room. It stopped every two or three minutes – and there was nothing wrong. The doors opened as if by magic. Peothe train hurtled on to stop again and again. He was carried to poured out and scrambled in. The doors closed the next level on a moving stairway. On the street he was surrounded by noise, people, cars and buses. Everyone was in a hurry. They even walked up the moving stairway.

She kept up a flow of information about the city and questions about his home. His responses to her were monosyllabic. She talked too much. She could not hold his interest.

He dozed off on the train, trying not to lean too close to her. He woke to find her arm cradling his head. But he did not feel safe with her. There was something of the hardness of Armah's body missing when she held him. She was too young.

The house she took him to had a neat compact garden in front. She showed him a room that was to be his own. Left alone, he placed the cotton handkerchief under his pillow and slept.

In the morning he woke and slipped out of the house. He found a bottle of milk on the doorstep, and no sun in the sky. He walked to the back of the house but could not find a trace of blue in the sky. A long plot at the back had been dug over.

He asked her, 'What are you growing at the back?'

'Just weeds,' she said.

'What about seeds?'

'Seeds take up too much space.'

'There's space at the back.'

'I mean inside.'

He was baffled by this reply. She did not think of telling him that seeds were planted in pots and then put outside.

She took him to the park and played with him on the grass. She bought him toys. At night she read to him from illustrated books about fairies, witches and magicians. But when she turned off the light and left him alone, he lay in his bed in the dark with the seed in its cotton handkerchief under his pillow, re-membering Armah and the still, bright landscape of his home.

One day he asked, 'Do you have any jewels?'

'Not valuable jewels,' she laughed.

'Do you have any jewels from home?'

'No.'

He could not bring himself to ask her if she knew Armah's story about the seed; or if Armah had also given her a seed. So he maintained some distance from her. Whenever he was alone he would remove the handkerchief from the top drawer in his room and spread it on the carpet. He had travelled all the way from Armah to his mother with the handkerchief spread before him. He was not like the thief because Armah had given him the seed when she kissed him goodbye. Nor was he like the planter who had removed the seed from the soil. If he was neither planter nor thief, what should he do with the seed? Should he place the seed in a glass box or wear it as a ring? He should have asked Armah, but she had been crying.

They lived like this for two months in the house, the young woman carefree and the boy maintaining his distance from her, unable to call her 'mother'. At night when longing welled up in him for the comfort of the old woman's arms, the warmth of the fire, and the stories created around the fireside, he hardened himself against such weakness, holding back the tears. She had chosen to live here, he had not. They had decided he should live here. He had not.

Then one day a plain white card was slipped through the letter-box and landed on the red carpet. She rushed around the house hiding everything that belonged to him. She packed all his clothes into a suitcase, picked up every toy and bit of toy that she could find; packed all these into plastic carrier bags which she then locked in the garden shed. She stripped his bed down to the mattress; the bedding was folded away in the airing cupboard; she even packed his pyjamas away each morning so that his room appeared unoccupied. All the curtains were kept drawn during the day, even the one across the front door. This routine she stuck to with scrupulous attention to detail. When the doorbell rang he knew as if by instinct that he should tiptoe out the back door. 'Is he the Group Areas man?' he whispered on his way out. It puzzled her. Did he imagine they were still in South Africa?

She opened the door and stood there in the manner of a thief who opens the door to the proprietor. And with the air of a proprietor, the man confronted her without speaking a word. He knew who she was. She had approached him personally for a house. He knew to whom the house was let. He was the housing officer. He had both the power to provide her with a house, and to evict her.

Without a word he stepped past her through the door, down the passage into the kitchen and without any preamble began opening cupboards, drawers, the oven, the grill, and the pantry door. She stood to one side of the kitchen with her back to the two mugs of steaming tea on the worktop.

He walked into the lounge, ran his finger across the polished table top, looked fixedly at the carpet then turned to go upstairs. She followed him mutely.

Halfway up the stairs, she suddenly remembered the toothbrushes, and could not recall if she had put the boy's away. She could only reassure herself when the man moved out of the bathroom doorway, that she had.

She was afraid he would notice the suitcase alongside the wall in one bedroom. He seemed to ignore it. He was almost through inspecting the house. She had nothing to fear now except that he would ask when she would vacate the house to the students to whom the unversity had let it. Then he seemed to pause more than was necessary in what was the child's room. She knew it was as empty as the spare bedroom, and worried about what could have caught his interest. She turned from the room, not wishing to look inside, not knowing what he would say.

He remained silent, giving her a false sense of security. He descended the stairs, at a casual, leisurely pace, then paused to look up at the curtain which had come down from the rail, and reached up to slide it back.

'I couldn't reach it,' she mumbled.

Reaching up to slide the curtain back, and without looking at her, he said, 'You don't happen to have your child with you, do you?'

'Oh, no. I wouldn't dream of doing that,' she said with a clear note of shocked disapproval in her voice.

'The university doesn't cater for women with children. You know that.'

She should have remained silent, after all, she had broken university regulations about sub-letting. Yet, she could not allow the opportunity to pass. 'But the university accepts registration from women with children. What does it expect us to do with our children?'

'That's not for me to say. The university is geared to the needs of teenagers. You'll be hearing from me.'

He left the front door wide open and she was alone. She ran up the stairs to the child's room to find out what the man had seen. On the bedside cabinet, perched with a distinct air of provocation, was a child's pair of cricket boots.

She did not know what the boots signified. He did not play cricket. She did not recall that he had a pair of cricket boots. Why had he put them there? What did it mean to him? Would he be able to explain to her, or would she have to wait until he was older? Would he have forgotten, by then?

Jellymouse

I was attempting to hold my own as a single mother, alienated from extended family and friends, while safeguarding the imaginative world my children were living in.

The moment each son approached seven, I watched him hover between a fragile space of living toys and the place where shattered glass was forbidden and impossibe to reshape. I wanted to delay each child's progress into the real world for as long as possible, only to discover I was unready for it myself.

It was Lusani's turn to hover at this point – Sinowa was eight, Wande ten – when we moved to a new house. The location contained a mix of colonial and English people, and we were South African. Yet the struggles to reach this point gave me a glorious sense of renewal. We would celebrate.

They spent their days running wild, discovering things, tumbling into the house, talking excitedly, squabbling to be the one to tell me. Football field. Swings. Slide. Rusty roundabout. Ice cream man in a van, not on a tricycle. A mad dog jumping at them. Hens in a hen house. Bushes that sting. They located school, chippie, fishing spot, country lanes leading to tadpoles, birds' nests, and a tree that made a wonderful den, in the days I took to unpack, leaving the front door wide open just in case the local gang proved hostile.

At night we slept on the floor, together, huddled under one quilt, talking about how Father Christmas would know where we had moved to; what he does if there's no chimney. When the wind blew, the windows flew open, and I had to be the one to go bravely to shut them.

And then we were all jolted into the real world by an early morning visit from our landlord. He was not checking to see how

we were settling in. He said several used cans of paint and old
settees had been dumped in a public area nearby. Someone he
could not name reported I dumped the items there.

I was staving off the pressure on my eldest son to assume the
role of man of the house. It meant keeping certain things from
him, not taking him into my confidence, and yet not sending
him away just then, as it would heighten his awareness that we
were being harassed. With the children looking on I joked with
the landlord, 'We could do with a couple of settees. You can see
we've none. Won't you give me a hand?'

He went away leaving us quiet and subdued for the first time
since our arrival. The carefree spirit they brought with them to
this place was as if slapped away. It seemed a good time for that
celebration.

But Wande demanded evidence of what we had to celebrate.

'We're celebrating something you can't see!' I said.

'Is that why the windows are too high?' he asked. 'What don't
you want us to see?'

'You must imagine the view.'

'I want a house with cupboards. And an attic.'

'We'll buy cupboards. Stop grumbling. Who's the party for?'

But all our birthdays were past – I'm Gemini, Wande is Leo,
Sinowa is Cancer, Lusani is Aquarius – so we agreed to celebrate
Lusani's pretend birthday. They were the invited guests. No
presents were expected. It would be a good party – provided
Lusani remembered not to expect any presents. Hovering on the
brink, he might believe it was really his birthday.

They had to be chased out to play – already they were finding
excuses to stay home to protect me – while I prepared for the
party and waited for the gas man. With a nice sticky mix of
margarine and flour on my hands – the mixer was at the bottom
of a crate – the sugar could not be found.

I rushed to the supermarket in our twelve-year-old car.
Halfway down the road the sounds of odd banging moved along
with my progression down the road. I wound down the window,
saw a group of people laughing, looking as if they had been
waiting for me to drive my car, and got out. There was a thick
chain tied around the axle. It had a notice board at one end.
One of the laughing men actually came to unwind the chain.

I was hostile and bristling, by the time I entered the

supermarket. Here, there was not a single foreign face – at the checkouts, or doing any shopping. And the staff immediately took turns following me around the store. I smiled first in my bright, hail-fellow-well-met, I-haven't-nicked-a-farthing-in-my-life way. It failed. It must have been obvious to other shoppers I was being followed, if I could detect it. A uniformed security guard brushed close by me several times. If I turned, a woman would rush away from somewhere close behind me. I found the sugar, went to the checkout and three members of staff converged around me. I was unsure what to do in such a situation.

The chain damaged the exhaust. The silencer was now ineffective. The gas man had been and left in the short spell that I was out. I was faced with the prospect of paying for a second call out.

With the cake in the oven, I ran to the telephone booth to phone round for a plumber to plumb in the washing machine.

'You want sixty-five pounds to plumb a washing machine? It cost me fifty! And if it goes next to the kitchen sink? Will it be cheaper? But you said it's the pipes that cost! I can't pay someone sixty-five pounds to work for one hour! What do I need to do it myself? You will say that. It's doing you out of condom money! And the same to you, mate!'

But the plumber's merchant was helpful. He advised me about stand-pipes and waste-traps. I ran home to take some measurements.

The landlord's visit, by now forgotten, heralded the beginning of an onslaught. While measuring under the sink, a woman wearing a golliwog badge walked up to the front door demanding her child's baby walker. She was mildly abusive when I said my children could walk. Then a woman called to complain that her children's crayons and powder paints cost a lot of money. Did I think she was buying them for my kids to use? Another called to say the bucket on her son's go-cart was cracked. Wande was too big for the cart. He should not have got in it in the first place. He must have damaged it. I must repair it. Windscreen wipers and car aerials were damaged in the night – my sons must be the culprits. The communal keys were missing. I was keeping them for some criminal motive. The washing machines had been broken into. When I went to use the washing machine someone slipped coins into the machines on my behalf. A freezer had been cleared by thieves – we must have had a feast.

The humorous way I talked to the landlord that morning gradually gave way to fury when anyone approached the front door. All day I vacillated between keeping these incidents to myself, and warning the boys not to play with certain children.

When they returned home we locked the door. The marble cake was baked, cooling on the rack. A pizza was in the oven. And a black cherry jelly in the fridge. They did a 'Bisto kids' scene, inhaling the aromas. The marble cake always has a secret running through the centre: coconut stirred about with yoghurt, chocolate flake, even peanut butter and jam. I was not telling what the secret was that day.

They set the table, rushing from dining room to kitchen for cutlery, plates, real glasses; deciding who will sit where, who will have the largest of the unmatched glasses, who will pour the drinks, who will be served first; while I waited to hear the shattered glass, trying not to think about the past, or the next day, or what appeared to be a crass neighbourhood.

Wande was nominated to be in charge of the ceremony – marching to the table with the marble cake. He hung about, feeling dubious about this honour, suspecting the sponge was too heavy for me to carry.

The pizza was ready, waiting for a lump of mozzarella to be grated over it. In the process of taking it to the dining room, we heard Wande, about to pick up the marble cake, let out a sound like a wailing siren. 'Mu-um!'

Expecting to see him disappearing down the sink hole, we charged into the kitchen only to find him standing there staring at the marble cake, with a fresh long, deep furrow down the centre – as if a mole had been burrowing underground. A thief had been here.

Each of us looked accusingly from one face to the next. At that moment even I was a suspect. Then my glance fell on Lusani, with real tears in his eyes, his mouth full of something, and cake crumbs around his lips, turned to stone. The others too seemed to be under some spell of enchantment. No-one moved or spoke. As long as they remained silent, Lusani could not swallow what was in his mouth. If he was expected to speak, it would be a dead giveaway.

The tension proved too much for him. Without any prompting, struggling to speak with his mouth full, he said, 'Not me.'

His denial was not strong, but there was a distinct sense he was disappointed that all suspecting eyes were focused on him. I awarded him ten out of ten for effrontery, struggling to handle this in a way that was not unfair to Wande who was learning about owning up if he did something wrong, and yet not propel Lusani into feelings of guilt.

Turning to question Sinowa, I asked, 'Where were you when I was bringing the pizza to the table?'

Wande made little attempt to hide his incredulity. He grabbed my arm, shaking me vigorously, 'Mum, look at Lusani!' I pretended he was a gnat and took a swipe at him.

The pressure eased off Lusani. He swallowed what he had in his mouth while Wande looked dismayed, not believing I missed seeing the evidence around Lusani's mouth.

'Do you think Sinowa is innocent, Wande?' I asked.

'If you question him, there must be more to this than meets the eye,' Wande said, and turning to Lusani asked, 'Why does she suspect Sinowa? Is he your accomplice?'

But Lusani, like a professional, had declared his innocence and refused to say any more. He simply shook his head very, very slowly.

'What about you, Wande? You found the cake. How do we know you're not the culprit?'

Wande, priding himself on being an ace detective, had solved all the codes in the *Super Sleuth's Handbook*, but reckoned he could not fathom how I was doing my sleuthing.

'Why aren't you questioning Lusani?'

We sat down at the table. It was hardly like a celebration to us. We sang 'Happy Birthday' in very subdued voices. 'Hip, hip, hooray!' sounded tearful. Then everyone was quiet. I calmly served the pizza. They prefer curry and rice, every one of them, but I would lose my skill in making bread and pastry, without practice. So they had to eat foreign food once a week and at celebrations.

Perhaps because I did not interrogate Lusani, he felt he stood accused. Whatever the reason, he repeated, without prompting, 'It wasn't me.'

None of us paid any attention to this remark. 'How's the pizza?' I asked.

'It wasn't me,' Lusani said, sounding a little cross. 'I didn't do it.' And gradually he became more and more cross and sulky. It seemed the more he denied it, the more he came to believe he was innocent.

As the meal progressed the animosity that Lusani felt at being silently accused began to envelop Sinowa. Even I could not understand how this happened.

'This food tastes horrible! Awful! I wish I didn't have to eat it!' Sinowa said.

Every word Sinowa said, Lusani repeated. 'Yes. It's horrible food! Must we eat it?'

They pushed their food about on the plate, but I noticed they continued eating. Sinowa was more cross with me for suspecting Lusani, even though I had not questioned Lusani at all.

'What about when we serve the cake and jelly?' Wande asked, very pleased at the possibility this presented for him.

'Yes, won't you be having cake and jelly?' I asked, but my voice sounded too sweet.

They knew I was up to something. The prospect of forfeiting cake and jelly had not occurred to them. They began giggling. The mood at the table lightened. The result was that Sinowa took on Lusani's defence. He turned in a kindly, caring way to Lusani and asked, 'Did you do it, Lusani?'

Slowly, with great deliberation, as if emphasising the certainty of his innocence, Lusani moved his head from side to side. This testimony was all Sinowa needed to be convinced Lusani was innocent. They repeated this question and answer routine, each time Sinowa referring to Lusani directly, 'Did you do it?' and receiving a firm, wide-eyed, 'No!' Sinowa then affirmed his kid brother's truthfulness. 'You see? He's telling the truth.'

The two of them stayed loyal to each other, performing this question and answer tactic until the pizza plate was scraped clean, with Wande sensing that there was something between them but unable to fathom what it was. They cleared the table while I sat quietly pondering some very deep thoughts.

Then I served the marble cake, with them eyeing the chocolate and nuts dripping from the centre. All three accepted their portions with a mumbled 'Thank you' and quickly gobbled it up. Silently they held out their plates and accepted a second helping while I went to the fridge to bring the black cherry jelly myself, since the mould was cold and slippery. A few seconds later I placed the jelly calmly on the table and they stared astonished at a hollow the size of a dessertspoon marring the smooth, wobbly surface.

They were shocked. I, believing in ghosts, fairies, and *Doppelgängers*, sat there placid and calm, like a fat frog waiting to be turned into a prince.

Wande chose this moment to tell me, 'Mum, someone hit Lusani today.'

'Who?' I asked, assuming it was a child's fight.

'A woman.'

'What d'you mean a woman? What woman?'

'I don't know her.'

'A woman hit Lusani and you didn't come home and tell me? Wande! What were you doing? Where were you?'

'We were playing Tig.'

'Then? What happened?'

'She just came to us and slapped Lusani.'

'Why Lusani? Why not you?'

'I don't know.'

'And she picked you up and shook you, hey Lusani?' Sinowa said, to Lusani.

They stared dismally at the jelly with its marred surface, while I planned another move. Before we moved here, I made excuses for them, whether they were colonial, or English. They were not to blame. They were conditioned by stereotypes. Dishonest Arab. Dirty Indian. Loose women. Sly. Cunning. Shady deals. Illegal anything. I made excuses for them. What chance did we have to trust? Leave it to the young generation. They will not have our hangups. It will be easier for them. Wait for this generation to die out. But that day something happened. I gave up on them. Perhaps I hoped – a black South African family would never be treated like this, anywhere else in England. It said something for England. From that day I refused to behave as if South Africa had never happened. For that was where they were at. Colonials and English expected me to transplant from South Africa and to meet them as if the burden of reconciliation was not on them.

Wishing fervently to diminish the effect of a strange adult beating a child, I wanted equally to be violent against this woman, against these people who would discredit us, against those who harassed us from day to day. On the outside I spoke about non-violence to the children. About Gandhi coming to help us in South Africa. About my grandfather fearing I would never be given a passport because he had been imprisoned with Gandhi in Bloemfontein.

They drew me back to their world. Sinowa, believing he had trapped the culprit, asked, 'Did you do this, Mum?'

Wande, trying to establish a motive, asked, 'Why did you do this, Mum? Are you trying to get revenge? Or are you trying to confuse the guilty person?'

'If Mum nibbled the jelly, she must have nibbled the marble cake,' Sinowa explained in an aside to Lusani.

The new development seemed like a perfect job for Wande's detective handbook. He slipped from the chair and dashed into his bedroom. I waited until he returned. The incident with the woman had taken second place. Still I felt I must teach them, when they are older, never to tolerate an attack on their person.

While Wande sat flipping through his book, I said with a very straight face, 'There must be a mouse in the fridge.'

At this stage, even Wande with all his experience of solving crimes was thrown off the track. The fridge is a piece of junk we picked up for a fiver. In winter it froze over like a freezer. Could a mouse possibly be living somewhere at the back? It feels very hot when they retrieve their marbles. Wande scrutinised my face to see if he could detect a hint of a smile, or guilt, perhaps. But my face was inscrutable.

I continued, 'And the mouse must've nibbled the cake. Sorry Lusani. You were innocent all the time.'

We sat staring at the jelly. 'This looks like the work of some very professional criminal, to me,' Wande said.

Instead of serving the jelly I began speculating aloud. 'What will we do, because mice carry germs and things? We'll all be sick because the cake is eaten.'

They looked from one to the other, each of them trying to take in the situation. 'What a good thing we haven't eaten the jelly!' I said.

Wande realised I was waiting for someone to own up. But

neither Lusani nor Sinowa responded. I went a step further. 'I wonder what poison we can use to kill the mouse?'

Lusani's eyes opened wider. Wande began playing my game.

'Remember Rahat said some poison makes the mouse want to eat more and more and more.'

'That's very cruel for the mouse.'

Then Sinowa asked, 'Yes, but what about getting ill from the cake?'

'Doesn't the smallest get ill first? Do you feel ill Sinowa? Or you Lusani?' I asked.

'Not yet,' they both chimed in together.

'I think the best thing to do is first throw the jelly away before someone forgets and eats it,' I said.

Sinowa and Lusani looked very disappointed with this suggestion. But still neither of them owned up. So I picked up the jelly and moved determinedly to the kitchen. Just as I was about to step through the door Lusani said, very formally, 'Excuse me! Are you telling the truth about the mouse?'

He was still hovering on the brink. What could I do but bring the jelly back to the table and hug him. He did not understand what he had said to bring about this response from me. But Wande did.

'I don't understand how you solved this case, Mum. Have you been secretly reading my detective handbook?' he asked.

I put out a note in the milk bottle with my first order, locked the door and drew the curtains to shut out the neighbours, hoping that tomorrow the milkman would be whistling and the postman would wish me 'good morning'.

Maths

It was harder for Sylverani to achieve equal status with her daughter than with her son.

The daughter was English-educated. When the mother is from peasant stock, first generation immigrant, speaking English with an accent, sending her children to school in England is a problem. They come home speaking posh. They copy. They feel shame about your dance, your music, your food even. What to do? We are here. Here they get brashness, like cocks crowing at midday. It's English schools to blame. Thank God it wears off.

Sylverani was nonconformist Indian. She refused to be a docile cook, cleaner or sexual partner. But she had a mulish streak. It made her persist in wearing a sari, while her son and daughter were at an impressionable age, while they were yearning for acceptance by their English mates. Yes, she could cut her hair when Prem offered to pay, but wearing a plait when girls have shaved heads, is that not resistance? Is that not strength? Why change on the outside to make things easy for them? Or for yourself even?

Prem was too young to be gracious. Throughout high school she would not be caught dead with Sylverani on the high street. Saragan, the son, was not so harsh. Boys love their mothers. Boys have heart. All women should have sons. Men, daughters.

As Prem was automatically promoted through school – a system for creating dumbkopfs Sylverani said – Prem came to have no concept of woman's intelligence. Who can blame the girl? The men are teaching the hard subjects. The women teach English. What can the girls do but idolise the men, despise the women and do badly in science and maths? To be equal with men, a girl had to be good at men's subjects. But poor Prem was hopeless at maths. Maybe if you stayed two years in the same form you would learn what the teacher was saying when you were writing love letters to that stupid boy with the big bones, Sylverani said. But no, Prem was preparing to leave school still idolising her brother. Saragan was brilliant at this and brilliant at that. He was taller. Stronger. And, she said, smarter than Sylverani. That's what English school did for Prem. Sylverani secretly thought Saragan's maths was shaky. If the teacher teaching maths was promoted every year, what to do?

When Prem was thirteen Sylverani worked·out their pocket money giving Saragan more, saying, 'Saragan is seventy-three pence older than you.' Prem swore that was a stupid way to reckon. More so since the reckoning was done by a woman who wore a sari in England, stayed home week in and week out, and never had a paying job. Because Saragan could not crack the formula, Sylverani's calculations had to be wrong.

Seventy-three pence did not go into the difference in their ages, in hours, days, months, or years; it did not go into their birthdays, into the number of letters in their names, the star signs under which they were born, nor even the place. But the reckoning meant seventy-three pence more for Saragan. What is more, Sylverani said any baby born out of wedlock to either of them would receive seven pence, as soon as it could count to thirteen.

The jokes about motherhood were a mistake. They made Prem clamour for leather, for metal objects, for cigarettes, everything symbolising the man's world. To be equal, Prem refused to think of herself as a woman.

Sylverani kept her fingers crossed, expecting a head-on collision. She waited while Prem competed aggressively for entrance into technology, fighting for acceptance as 'one of the boys' in her drinking preferences, her way of dressing, her attitude to things in the home. She listened to Prem blaming women's status on their failure to cast off responsibility for others. Big words. Big ideas. What would she do with a little baby on her hands? And she experienced at first hand Prem's contempt for women who placed their children's interests before their own. Here Sylverani pleaded guilty.

She knew she was losing the battle. What to do to get respect, stuck in the house like a dhurry?

Prem and Saragan neared school-leaving age. And the pocket money business became a formula they carried over into other areas. They used it to prove Sylverani could not argue logically; her memory for facts and figures had to be challenged; she was out of touch with the world; she could not have an opinion, especially not on current affairs. From this premiss they grew more and more bold, until, deciding they should give her the benefit of their English education, they began demanding an account of the bills, and the bank statements, and even offered ways to economise on food.

Stimulated by these challenges, Sylverani grew intellectually fit arguing with them. But once they resorted to challenging mundane household things, she rapturously treated herself to the freedom a man has sharing a house with strangers. Prem and Saragan came home to last night's dishes stacked in the sink, the carpet unhoovered, the glasses, yoghurt cartons, ice cream papers lying just where they had left them: on the floor in the sitting room, and under the armchairs; plates stuck together in the bedroom. She demonstrated how the washing machine worked then stopped doing their laundry. The sewing machine was dragged from under the bed, threaded, and left in an accessible spot, all ready for use. And then it was a simple matter to wait for them to murmur, 'Aren't we eating?' at eleven o'clock at night, before pointing to the frying pan and wishing them goodnight.

When people called round, stepping straight into the kitchen, casting disapproving glances that swept along the worktops, Sylverani trembled. She thanked God no-one was trying to arrange a second marriage for her. Some rolled up their sleeves and set to washing the dishes. Others refused a cup of coffee, with pursed lips. One member of her own sex muttered, 'Lazy woman!' And an indoctrinated girl-child asked, 'Auntie, why are there always dishes on the table?' Sylverani was embarrassed – on their account. For no-one could see the point she was making.

She wanted more than to be equal with men. She wanted no woman, whether because she was young, educated, with money, opportunity or whatever, to feel superior to her. Yet Prem was the younger, educated, opportunist woman, defending her equality with men, and discarding her mother as another category of woman. And women, up and down the country, do they not still wait hand and foot on able-bodied teenagers?

Then Sylverani had a lucky break. It came with their reports that year. It said Prem had to drop maths. Saragan would fail maths if he did not make an 'extra effort'. Prem needed no persuasion that Sylverani, and not their truant father, contributed the gene that gave her this maths handicap. It was the opportunity Sylverani needed to win respect. That Saturday she announced, 'When we finish with the car, you've got a maths lesson.'

They moaned. 'Not again!'

'First she helps us with English. Then science. Now maths. When will this woman give up on us?'

Sylverani chastised them. 'I never talk like this in front of my mother. Where you hear children talking like this in front of their mother?' she asked. They said their friends do. Worse. You should hear them.

'Anyhow, I don't need maths,' Saragan said.

Prem added, 'Nor me.'

'Everyone needs maths!' she said.

'Einstein didn't!' Saragan replied.

They winked at each other believing, together, they had put a cork on it. Sylverani went to collect the mail and to check the car had not been sabotaged in the night. It was safe so she emptied the bucket she kept handy for an attack. There was a cessation of hostilities during the football match. Then they helped work on the car. Sylverani had progressed from simple, mundane jobs like draining the oil, and changing the oil filter and spark plugs, to working on the cooling system and then the brakes. But even at seventeen Prem could find nothing to admire about this. So, with Sylverani grousing on one side, Saragan and Prem grumbling on the other, she never finishing a sentence, the two giving her back chat, she assuming they know exactly what each unfinished thought means, they tormenting her by providing the wrong endings – they worked on the car.

'It was the way his moustache curled under his nose.'

'Moustache? Whose moustache, mother? Some weirdo been hanging around the house?'

'It made scenes from the *The Jewel in the Crown* flash before my eyes.'

Saragan moaned, 'It's hard to act maturely when you're dealing with someone you can't do a karate chop on.'

'Your teacher. He wanted me to toodle off and be a good girl while he got on with doing what a man's got to do.'

'Mother, you have too many things on your mind. Let me work on my own,' Saragan said.

'Me too,' Prem said. She usually had a hell of a lot to say, but at times like this, she echoed Saragan. It annoyed him, but it also made him feel he was the one to be reckoned with.

'It wasn't what he said,' Sylverani whispered, 'or the way he said it.'

'Mother, never mind. We'll work on our own.'

'I'm trying to help you, for God's sake! You're up against attitudes, children. Attitudes! By the time you understand what an attitude is, it'll be too late.'

'Mother, stop swearing. Think of the neighbours. They've never heard of an Asian woman swearing.'

'It's time we gave the neighbours a new stereotype.'

If one thing put the fear of God into Sylverani it was the threat of dropping out of school. They knew it.

'Miss Perkins thinks I won't get my A-levels,' Prem announced. 'I've a job interview.'

'Mistake Jeronimo!' Saragan whispered, 'You've removed the pin from a hand grenade.'

'A hundred years ago,' Sylverani began, and went into a spiel about kids forced to work. Dickens . . . Oliver Twist . . . his whole family living in a prison. People going to war to stop child labour. Children working in the mines. And here you are . . . hating school . . . wanting to go out to work.

'Mother,' he said, 'you didn't have all the privileges we have. We take education for granted.'

'Oh? Because I come from the Third World, hey? . . . You're not Indian, hey? You're English, hey? You despise me? You're lucky, hey? . . . to live in Britain? Your mother's deprived, hey? Disadvantaged, hey?'

Each time she said 'hey', she clobbered him – in a friendly, non-aggressive way. There was only one thing for them to do. 'Sorry, Mum,' they mumbled in unison.

They began the maths lessons, with the two of them trying to intimidate her. 'What about theorems? Inequalities? Statistics?' Saragan said.

'I've told you children . . . time and again who draws up these syllabuses. Snobs. Academic snobs who want to keep some subjects for the snobs. Teaching research biology to O-level pupils! Imagine?'

One week later they were coming along fine. But they hated being taught by a parent.

'Teachers are there to be made fun of. The way they walk. The things they say. They way they dress,' Saragan grumbled.

'But what do we do when a parent is teaching?' asked Prem.

'Feel guilty. She brought you into the world, miss. She could've had an abortion!'

Then Sylverani made a mistake. She asked for a sheet of paper from the new pads she'd bought them, to work out an example. The shops were shut.

'I can't tear pages from this pad. Ask him.'

'Why not? It's a jumbo pad.'

'Destructiveness, Mother! Remember the holy words of wisdom?'

She was reluctant to force the issue, so she turned to Saragan.

'It's a new pad,' he said.

'Good for you,' Prem slapped him on the back. 'Unoriginal, but still, it shows resistance. You deserve to be left off,' she said, tearing out a page. 'Teachers ought to have their own paper.'

'You win some, you lose some. With her you've got to know when to say enough is enough. When to give in,' Saragan said.

Undaunted, Sylverani went on like that all week. One day a page from her. Next day a page from him. They said they were feeling lucky, not to have got to know her just yesterday. Now they knew all the tricks of survival in this adult world. So before week two was over Saragan objected to having lessons with his kid, meaning his sister. He did not have to say the words 'sibling rivalry', just let her imagination run wild.

'If I teach separately, it'll take up more of my time,' Sylverani said.

Prem could see he was on the right tack. This was just what she needed. The chance to be magnanimous. 'Then teach him. I don't need maths.'

'You both need maths. You both need extra lessons.'

'Can't you afford to pay someone?'

'Why pay someone? My maths is ten times better.'

'Mother!' Saragan exclaimed, 'You learnt maths before the Ancient Egyptians. There's such things as triangles and trigonometry, y'know.'

'Poor children!' Sylverani shook her head sadly, 'they don't know who invented maths. And to think you're at school in England.'

'You see, Prem. She is a survivor from Ancient Egypt.'

'Humour her,' said Prem.

When Sylverani needed to borrow a pen – she bought them three each – they suspected her of succumbing to their rivalries.

'She can't stand to see us hogging it all to ourselves,' Prem said.

'Let her use yours,' Saragan said. 'I don't lend to people who can't buy their own stuff.'

'You're using up all my ink,' Prem complained, feeling she had to assert her rights or she would be dominated.

Sylverani gave in. She bought her own paper and pens. So they concluded that assertiveness works.

'You're learning a great deal from us now we're in our teens and can argue with you, Mother.'

'You were having it all your own way while we were kids. We took everything you said like it was gospel. Remember the business about children not having nerves? I believed you! It really shook me when I learnt the truth. I lost a lot of confidence in you that day. Waiting for the nerves to grow.'

'Poor children! What they teach you at school?'

Then she suggested they begin each sum on a clean page.

'Whatever for? Wasting paper! God Almighty!'

It's practice. For the exams.'

'Wasting good clean paper,' Prem said. 'Think of all the trees!'

Again Sylverani felt they had a point.

'These women on their own bringing up kids. They need our point of view,' Saragan said.

'See how she listens to us now?' Prem said.

Then one afternoon Saragan came into the room very late. He started taking the mickey because Prem had been 'stuck here with old albatross' as they called Sylverani, while he had been cycling about. He poured himself a drink.

'Pour me one,' Prem said.

'Leave the drink alone,' Sylverani commanded. 'Come, sit down.'

'Teachers! A breed of dictators. No sense of democracy. We would out-vote you any day. That's why you keep reminding us parents remain parents to their children,' Saragan said.

He grumbled about living in a house where he was in the minority. He went about the kitchen slamming drawers and cupboard doors, mumbling and muttering under his breath about women in general. He refused to sit down till he had his drink. Sylverani was in a rage. Saragan began laughing and spluttering over his drink. His laughter was contagious. Prem laughed. Stopped. Laughed. Stopped. She could not control herself. Saragan was now coughing and choking. Sylverani was rampant. She stormed away, refusing to teach them ever again.

Prem hung about Sylverani's bedroom door saying she was sure she would fail maths. Saragan leaned against the chest of drawers looking apprehensive. Prem brought her cups of tea three times that day, but Sylverani refused to budge.

'I've had enough of being put down just because I'm someone's mother,' she said. 'Go on. Live up to your teachers' expectations of you. Prove them right! I'm finished with you two!'

Then Saragan apologised. Sylverani enthused about boys being all heart and today's girls being iron maidens. Prem said she thought an apology was going too far. Sylverani knew Prem would hold out longer. She mentioned something about leaving Saragan something in her will.

'Bribes, threats, blackmail. You use everything. You have no principles,' Prem said. 'Well, there is not much around here I can see worth inheriting. But one never knows.' So she apologised too, while Sylverani repeated the phrase, 'A hundred years ago . . .'

'Some people do not age. Must be some Egyptian method of preserving,' Prem said.

Their lessons resumed. Then one day there was a break-through. Prem solved an equation she had been struggling with for days. She was feeling really chuffed. She actually said she thought the lessons were paying off. Then Saragan came in. Late as usual. Grumpy. Prem bragged to him about how she solved a six-term expression. This made him want to attempt it himself. He wanted no help. Nor did he want to see the answer. He did it! And gave Sylverani all the credit for it. Hugging and kissing her until Prem complained.

'God Almighty! This is like something out of *Rumpelstiltskin*. The two of you dancing a jig all round the kitchen table. This is too much for me. Mother, Saragan is seventy-three pence older than me,' she said. 'I'll never say any different. And Mother, Saragan is the only hero I'll ever have.'

With these words Prem ended her conflict with Sylverani. By then she was eighteen, preparing to leave home.

The Story Teller

This is one version of a story which has come down to us with slight changes when told by different members of the family. It is only told after having extracted a promise that it be related to one's own children, and that they must make the same promise. But by the time we heard the story, we gave very little credence to it. This was because several members of that generation had inherited the yearning to tell a story which seemed so real, we needed to be told if it were true or not, and they never ever returned to say, I made it up. The truth of this story could be verified by going through the passenger lists of Lloyds shipping.

'We were a ragamuffin bunch of kids. No school to go to. Therefore no need for shoes. Nothing to do all day but play. If we had an idea to do a thing, we'd do it for weeks, and then suddenly it doesn't interest us any more, and we do something else. This time we were just frolicking in and out of the sea running by our village. We waited while the fishermen were pulling their nets to the boats. We helped them. There was a lot of noise and shouting. Then one by one they shoved off. They wouldn't take us with them. We chattered like monkeys, they said. We'd frighten the fish away.

'The beach was deserted. When we looked we saw a sailing ship out in the sea.

'There was Neela. She was the eldest. And Miti. Parbhoo. My brother, Pacha. Me. And others. We were inquisitive. Going in and out of every shrub and cave we found. We were too cheeky for Neela to control. We always ran away from the village before we could be given jobs to do. Though we didn't mind helping the fishermen because we wanted to be taken along with them, only they never wanted us with them. At the end of the day we went home wet and speckled with sea sand. Early next morning we returned, to see if the sea had washed away the shells we'd left in a circle.

'For days we saw the ship standing there, its outline, its masts and spars, like a skeleton stretching towards the sky. Because it seemed pasted into the sky, we played without thinking about it. It never moved.

'Then one day we stopped playing – how could we be interested in our game? Something was happening on the ship. We watched a rowing boat lowered from the side of the ship. They were clumsy. Someone in the boat fell out and had to swim out of the way before the boat splashed on to the water. When it touched the water, little people climbed down the ropes and into the boat and then they rowed and rowed towards the shore. When we saw the boat approaching we ran into the sea. We waved to the boat. We shouted to the rowers. Like a miracle they changed direction, and rowed towards us. We helped them pull the boat on to the sand like we had been waiting for them for years and years. Already we were acting as if the boat belonged to us. As if they were visitors we should take to our village.

'Maybe the oarsmen were English. We couldn't tell the difference. They went off into our village, leaving us to play in their boat, to take turns rowing, wielding a whip, keeping a look out, playing captain, and each and every one of us refusing to be a passenger.

'The sun was already down, and Neela was chattering and chattering about who was going to get the most hiding for not going home when she told us to. But no-one was afraid of Neela, or of her scolding. We would begin crying when we approached our village, even before anyone beat us. Just as soon as we saw the stick we'd start yelling. And everyone would be concerned to know what had happened to us.

'Then the ship men returned just as we were thinking of going to find them. They had an Indian man with them. At first they pushed the boat off the sand and then, as if they understood why we were watching them, the man asked if we wanted to go on board the sailing ship. What a thing! How could we say no? We were pushing and fighting to climb into the boat, in case there wasn't enough room for all of us. Only that Neela hung back.

She wanted us to wait while she ran home to ask Ayah. Ask Ayah! And what if Ayah wants to come too? How long will it take for Ayah to walk from the village? First Ayah must find her walking stick and then she can't leave the house until she makes some prayers.

'The ship men don't have time to wait. Even we knew that. They promised to bring us back in the time – they took out their watches – it would take Neela to run home and return – cross their hearts and hope to die.

'We didn't know about this promise. Just then Neela asked if we'd forgotten about ''Tapu'', the evil place from where no-one ever returns. We jumped out of the boat like it was on fire. Seeing we were so frightened, these men described the ship with long strides up and down the beach; and wide arms that picked each of us up and dumped us back in the boat. But we jumped out again. Like it was too hot for us. So they fenced with imaginary swords, and we believed the adventures and escapades they were acting were real. It was all on board the ship. They pushed away the babies who were afraid. They said they only let brave people on to their ship.

'Miti was called impudent. She was the first. She crossed the space separating us from the men and stood with one hand on her hip scolding us for having sheep's brains. She was thin with large boney knees and big black eyes. Talking about sheep's brains reminded me Ayah was cooking sheep's head that night. So I wanted to go home. Then Miti's sister stepped over to her side. Together they climbed into the rowing boat. Neela was shouting and screaming for us to come back home. But one by one we were shamed by the girls into needing to prove we were brave. Neela ran towards the path. We called her back. We begged her not to tell Ayah. But she wouldn't come. The Indian man went into a huddle with the ship men. And then we left him on the beach.

'We were rowed out to sea to touch the ship we had only ever seen from a distance; so we could brag when we returned home, that we have actually crossed the ocean.

'And these Englishmen kept their word. They allowed us to board their ship. They gave us a guided tour above the deck. They allowed us to touch the wheel; to scamper up and down the rope ladders; up into the crow's nest; to look out for land through the one-eyed telescope. Below the deck we ran freely about, peeping through port holes, retreating from the heat of the kitchen. And they gave us food.

'There were hundreds and hundreds of people on board. They looked really tired. Still they became angry when they saw us.

'But we said we were not travelling anywhere. We only came to have a look round the ship. The Indians carried us up on to the deck. While we were below deck, the ship had raised anchor. We were crying as we watched India going away from us.

'I told everyone we met, how we were tricked onto the ship. But the ship men, hearing me, said I was telling stories. They persuaded the Indians that my father was somewhere on board that very ship.

'We watched the moon growing full and disappearing, so many times. Then one day the ship docked at a place they called The Bluff. They told us this was South Africa.

'We stood in a long queue waiting to come off the ship. When it was my turn to speak to the official on the ground, with only my brother and no mother or father, I told them we were tricked. I thought they would send us back home. But they talked amongst themselves then told the others our parents must have died on the voyage from India. My brother and I were given a tin ticket for identification, and we were made to put our thumb print on a piece of paper. Then a man took us away to work on his farm. That's how I came to be here.

'I knew the time of year because the Europeans in Durban were preparing for a celebration. It was the eve of the Christian festival – Christmas.

'One day my brother stowed away on a ship, hoping it would take him back to India – it was destined for Australia. I never saw him again. I have never been home to India.'

And They Christened It Indenture

Many Muslims and Hindus refused baptism at the mission stations in Natal. Their interpretation of indentured labour emphasises that the architects were Christian.

Slavery had been abolished. But labourers were still required to sweat in the fields.

In those days people with money could persuade the government to believe anything. So the slave owners persuaded everyone that to progress from waking up in the morning to a field full of singing labourers who only cost one several strokes with the lash, to a queue of workers with outstretched hands at the end of every day, was as simple as making the sign of the cross.

Those who bid good money at the auctions for the strongest slaves swore they accepted with good faith their investments walking away from them. They even negotiated with the former unpaid workers to return and receive wages. After all, people who had worked without pay would be grateful for even a penny at the end of the day.

Except that the penny would not do. It bought a man a plate of food for one day. What of his wife and children?

Being reasonable people, the former slave owners thought seriously about how they could pay a labourer a penny and make it suffice for a month, or two, or three.

A brilliant person who wished to remain anonymous hit upon the brainwave that only men without wives and children should be employed.

The former slave owners ranged high and low throughout the Commonwealth searching for former slave men without wives and children. Unhappily, they found only one.

And then a genius appeared in their midst, who also did not wish to be remembered by historians. He said they should bring men from a foreign country without their wives and children.

But men throughout the Christian world had promised before God to cling to their wives. And baptised wives likewise had promised before God to cling to their husbands.

Then miraculously, another brilliant person appeared, this time as if sent by God Himself, who said that heathen men did not promise before God to cling to their wives. And heathen wives did not promise before God to cling to their husbands.

Low and behold, there they had the solution. It was so obvious to them. The country with the largest number of heathens in the world was our India.

Happily for the former slave owners, the natives of India were subdued by the British, the very same British who were in Natal and needed labour that would cost a penny.

And to add to the joy the Indians must have been so rich they welcomed the idea of working for a penny for the people who had owned slaves. They thanked God that they had not made promises before Him to cling to their wives. If they had, who would have come to the assistance of the former slave owners? But more than this, they thanked God that slavery had been abolished.

And mysteriously, although Indians had never left India before, and even though they believed that a Hindu is forbidden to cross the ocean, as if they were filled with the Holy Ghost they suddenly developed this inexplicable urge, like missionary zeal, to leave India.

And when they survived cholera, dysentery and typhoid, and after they resisted the impulse to throw themselves into the Indian Ocean, and they finally arrived at their destination, to be given in bondage to a master of indentureship – only then they understood, as clearly as they could not write their names, that although they belonged to a master, and could not move anywhere without that master's permission, they were certainly not slaves. For slavery had been abolished. And a bond is a man's word.

At night they sat around and marvelled at how well they were treated. They closed their ears to the story of the *Shah Allum*, whose captain and crew abandoned the burning vessel and left 399 Indian labourers to die. They laughed out loud when an official was designated 'Protector of Indian Immigrants'. And when their indentureship was over and they wished to return home they were not even disappointed to find they were expected to pay their own passage to India. And those who had married, and had children and grandchildren, thought it was an even bigger joke when they discovered their marriages were not recognised – Hindu and Muslim alike. And when they became old and lonely, and the prospect of returning to India was remote, and they sought to have their wives and children brought over, they applauded the arguments as to why their families should remain in India. And they knew that they were certainly not slaves. But more than this, they knew that a great change had come over the former slave owners.

So to demonstrate their faith in the idea that slavery had been abolished, some of them became Christians in order that their marriages could be recognised, their children become legitimate and inherit what they did not have to bequeath.

And those who had the means bought their freedom from the master, while others continually signed on again and again as indentured labourers, because they could not buy their freedom, nor could they pay their return passage to India. And they were eternally grateful to the masters for allowing them to sign on as indentured labourers, for where would the money have come from if they were paid in bags of rice?

And when they were told to pay a poll tax for their wives, sons and daughters over a certain age, they knew that when they paid the tax they would be allowed to walk on the pavements and not be pushed into the streets. So they gave up alcohol, they gave up cigarettes, they gave up meat. They crowded together in one family house. They hawked vegetables. They sold food to the unmarried workers in the field. They helped each other. And then they refused to pay the tax.

Notes

Daggha Or dagga, from the Khoi-San for the narcotic made from hemp (marijuana) and smoked as a cigarette.

Ijaar An Urdu word pronounced 'Ie-jar', used to denote the soft, baggy trousers worn by Muslim women with the chemise. The use of the word has remained unchanged since brought over from India, but is currently used in Bangladesh to describe an undergarment such as knickers.

Klaverjass A four-handed game of cards played by the Coloured and Indian communities.

Meid An Afrikaans word pronounced 'mate', literally means a young woman but used aggressively to suggest derogation.

Meisie An Afrikaans word pronounced 'may-see', meaning little girl. Since black women are called 'girl' even by white children, and since the word is Afrikaans, the use of 'meisie' by a black woman to a white one is a double attack.

Ngoma An African word for a celebration, which can include a naming ceremony.

Nyana A Xhosa word, meaning 'my son', or 'this is my son'.

Saamberani An Indian word, for the incense burnt when praying or when someone dies to keep the newly deceased spirit at rest.

Skelm Pronounced skellum, meaning a rogue.

Sluits An Afrikaans word for the erosion of the sandy paths and tracks caused by the rain, which with time become gullies.

Spek 'n Boontjes An Afrikaans phrase pronounced Spec-n-bwoonkiss, which literally means fat/lard and little beans, but the phrase is used to denote a young child playing any game with adults or older children, where the rules are relaxed so that the young child does not forfeit points, or is not out when she should be.

Tali A Tamil word for a small square of solid gold given to a bride by the bridegroom at a Hindu marriage ceremony and worn on a chain around the neck. Roman Catholic Indians arriving as indentured labourers in Durban in 1860 were allowed by Reverend Father Sabon OMI to wear the Tali instead of the wedding ring.

Tapu A Tamil word for a place over the sea to which anyone who disappeared was believed to have been taken.

Tata A Xhosa word – properly means 'father'. Tato Mkhulu means grandfather, and could be written Ntata, or loosely Tata. Tata is also used as a respectful form of address for any old man. It is more commonly used to denote grandfather, than father.

Tokoloshe Possibly derived from Khoi-San, pronounced Tock-o-loshie, used to denote something which is not so much a spirit as a tiny being, such as an imp, or elf, which is mischievous, has a sexual interest in young girls, and behaves intemperately.

THE AFRICAN WRITERS SERIES

The book you have been reading is part of Heinemann's long-established series of African fiction. Details of some of the other titles available in this series are given below, but for a catalogue giving information on all the titles available in this series and in the Caribbean Writers Series write to:
Heinemann Educational Publishers,
Halley Court, Jordan Hill, Oxford OX2 8EJ;
United States customers should write to:
Heinemann, 361 Hanover Street,
Portsmouth, NH 03801–3912, USA.

DENNIS HIRSON (ED)
The Heinemann Book of South African Short Stories

The issue of apartheid pervades this significant anthology of South African short stories with contributions from such celebrated writers as Bessie Head, Alex La Guma and Nobel Prize Winner, Nadine Gordimer.

MIA COUTO
Every Man Is A Race

A collection of Mozambican short stories by a writer whose first short story collection was variously described as 'lyrical', 'magical' and 'compassionate' by the reviewers. Mia Couto lives and works in Maputo and is a well-known poet and journalist.

STEVE CHIMOMBO
Napolo and Python

Napolo, the mythical serpent of Malawi, inspired the poems in this collection. Playwright, short story teller and critic, Steve Chimombo also teaches English at the University of Malawi.

BUCHI EMECHETA
Kehinde

A middle-aged Nigerian woman's need to lead her own life forces her to deal with the guilt surrounding her family ties and grow confident in the belief of her own dreams.

This is Buchi Emecheta's first novel for five years.

In The Ditch

A harrowing and humorous account of a young, lone, Nigerian mother's determination to carve a place for herself against the odds.

New Edition

Head Above Water

Buchi Emecheta's autobiography, spanning the transition from tribal childhood in the African bush to life in North London as an internationally admired author.

New Edition